Sworn to Lead

SWORN TO LEAD

Sworn Navy SEALs Romance

Charlee James

TULE
PUBLISHING

Sworn to Lead
Copyright© 2024 Charlee James
Tule Publishing First Printing, March 2024

The Tule Publishing, Inc.

ALL RIGHTS RESERVED

First Publication by Tule Publishing 2024

Cover design by LLewellen Designs

No part of this book may be used or reproduced in any manner whatsoever without written permission except in the case of brief quotations embodied in critical articles and reviews.

This is a work of fiction. Names, characters, places, and incidents are products of the author's imagination or are used fictitiously. Any resemblance to actual events, locales, organizations, or persons, living or dead, is entirely coincidental.

AI was not used to create any part of this book and no part of this book may be used for generative training.

ISBN: 978-1-962707-04-6

Dedication

For Jack S.
The purest form of sunlight

Dear Readers,

I'm so excited to introduce you to a new series, and hope that you enjoy Brynn and Neo's story. Like I do in my own life, Brynn and Neo care for a medically complex child. This journey is often one of many varying emotions: love, fear, joy, advocacy, trauma, and celebration. Everyone's experience is different, just as every individual is unique. Spending extended amounts of time in hospitals and working with those who have profound challenges has highlighted the resiliency of children and adults living with disabilities. Throughout this book, I emphasize some of the wonderful moments of loving a person who has a disability, but this in no way is meant to diminish the hurdles faced by individuals or the people who love them and provide them support.

The endless emergency room visits and extended inpatient stays. Hours spent on the telephone advocating for necessary medical supplies, ensuring IEPs and 504s are in place for in-school support, and coordinating therapies and treatments. Nights spent in a bedside chair, jarred by every blip on the monitor. The overwhelming fear and heartache of loving someone you might lose too soon.

But through the obstacles, there is light. We celebrate each milestone hard and cherish each birthday a little harder. We make deep connections with other families on similar paths. Together, we join to raise awareness, promote inclusion, and offer support. This journey can be isolating. Lonely. It can also open your heart to an entire community of those fighting big battles.

To all those who love someone diagnosed with a disability or who has a disability, you are not alone.

With much love,
Charlee James

CHAPTER ONE

Neo "Ransom" Godfrey stared blankly at the death notification in his hands and felt nothing. Maybe if he were a better person, a better son, he'd have mustered a twinge of remorse. The stirrings of sadness, something a son should experience when informed of a parent's death, were absent. There was just…nothing inside the hollow of his chest. For as long as he could remember, his mom had reminded him he was a cold bastard like his father. She hadn't been wrong. So when his commander called him into the barracks from training to tell him the woman who had raised him overdosed and drove into a brick wall, he didn't flinch.

His late mother's lawyer had requested his presence in Boston to go over the terms of her estate. Returning to the wealthy Boston suburb of Weston was not on his list of preferred activities. He'd enlisted the moment he turned eighteen and hadn't seen the woman who gave birth to him in fifteen years, let alone the place he grew up. Any money she'd left him was not wanted, especially if it would save him from visiting the lonely manor where he grew up. Tagging his phone off the bureau, he dialed the number at the bottom of the notice, content to tell the lawyer thanks but no thanks.

His SEAL team had been prepping for an overseas mission. One he wouldn't derail because of his mother's poor choices. Speaking of the Teams, his came filtering into his apartment. Julian "Joker" Desmond, Hunter "Branch" Green, and Archer "Silver" Ross were his brothers. Had saved his sorry ass more times than he could count, but damn if they weren't homing pigeons zeroing in, wanting to know why he was pulled from their training exercise. The couch dipped when Branch sat at the other end. The fridge opened and closed. Glass bottles clanked together as Silver came into the room carrying four cold ones. Joker sat with his arms crossed and a typical scowl slashed across his face. None of the men cared that they were invading his privacy, or that he was on the phone. They cared, and that felt damn good.

"Sullivan and Fletcher." He moved the phone away from his ear at the overly bright tone of the receptionist.

"Hubert Sullivan, please." Manners and etiquette had been drilled in long ago by his grandparents. One of the very few lessons taught to him by blood. Once they died, their train-wreck daughter hemorrhaged their fortune partying with the elite while he languished away in a luxurious hell at the tender age of eight.

"He's entertaining a client at the moment." The click of nails on a keyboard was audible.

"This is Neo Godfrey returning his request." He rolled his eyes at her quick intake of breath.

"My apologies, Mr. Godfrey," the receptionist stammered. "He just became available." That exact response was the reason he loved the fuck out of Virginia. No one knew about his family's fortune. What was left of it anyway. He had his own trust fund from his grandmother, something he hadn't dipped into much. His mother, on the other hand, well…a cocaine habit wasn't cheap.

He switched his phone to speaker so he wouldn't need to explain the conversation to his brothers and grabbed the bottle Silver had set on the table. Condensation iced his calloused fingers.

"Mr. Godfrey, this is Mr. Sullivan. Please accept my condolences. Such a tragic loss." The man's voice was deep and muffled, like he was talking through a mouthful of cotton.

His jaw hardened. A tragic loss is one you didn't expect. His mother had her fair share of chances and luck, and it had run out. "I'd prefer to tie up loose ends over the phone or via email."

"I'm afraid this sort of information is best shared in person. Your mother left you—"

"It doesn't matter," he said, cutting the man off. Maybe the manners his grandparents had pushed on him weren't that well honed after all. "I'll have my lawyer draft up a request to donate any funds left to me to Boston Children's Hospital."

There was silence on the other end of the line. The lawyer cleared his throat. "It burdens me to share that your mother left nothing of monetary value to you or your sibling."

His breath caught. A slug to the chest of his Kevlar tactical vest. Static roared in his ears, blocking the drone of the man's voice. "Stop." The command was sharp on his tongue.

"Did you say sibling?" He glanced around the room at his teammates' furrowed brows and troubled expressions.

"Yes. Your brother. You're the next of kin, but given his medical complexities, it's natural to look for other options. There are some state facilities—"

A growl of frustration ripped through him. "There's nothing natural about abandoning your sibling. You've dealt with Shae Godfrey, so I'll look past your mention of state facilities, but do not clump me into the same category as that leech. Where the hell is my brother right now?" God, had his mother stooped so low that she'd give away her own child because it was more convenient than dealing with whatever medical challenges he had going on? His stomach hardened to the point of pain.

"I don't think you grasp the scope of those medical complexities. Mrs. Godfrey left him in the care of a live-in nurse, but the estate was sold to pay off a substantial debt last year. Jacob is thirteen years old and requires around-the-clock care due to spastic quadriplegia, a severe type of cerebral palsy. The school system reported that he was withdrawn from special education services due to a move. Several departments are trying to locate him."

Bile burned up the back of his throat. His brother. His brother was missing.

"On it," Silver muttered, crossing the room. One glance at Silver's face and Neo knew his teammate was handling what the jerk on the phone couldn't. He was calling in some favors from the tech guys.

"Forward me the guardianship paperwork. I'll expect it within the next hour." He hung up the phone without waiting for a reply. They'd find Jacob. A knot had twisted in his gut, churning and writhing with years of suppressed anger. Of all the rotten things Shae Godfrey had done to him, keeping the knowledge of his sibling from him was by far the worst. Thirteen years lost. Fuck.

Two days. Forty-eight hours. Two thousand eight hundred and eighty minutes. That's how long it had taken to track down his brother's address and catch a flight to Boston. He hailed a cab outside the airport, not bothering to check into a hotel first. He paid the driver and tried to tamp down his growing ire. His mom had pissed away millions, and his brother was the one who had paid for it by having to move into the shitty shambles of an apartment building looming in front of him. Now she was dead, and who the hell knew who'd been taking care of Jacob.

The kid hadn't exactly hit the jackpot in the brother department either. He'd never been good with children. As a matter of fact, he wasn't good with people in general. He cared about his team, but they'd been through hell together. Seen things the general population would never have to. Neo was cold and hard. Not exactly the caring role model his younger brother deserved, but the mere thought of not stepping up to provide for his own blood was abhorrent. He had a duty to his sibling. If one hair on the boy's head had been harmed, he'd go nuclear. His commander had given him an emergency two-week leave, and he wasn't wasting a second of the time.

There was a lot to do in a short period, but his first order of business was getting Jacob out of this monstrosity of a building. Anger clawed up his chest, gripping his throat when he opened the unsecured front door. More when the stairs nearly splintered beneath his weight. When he noticed the dangling smoke detector in the long hallway, he resolved to file a complaint with the city. He scowled at the door of the listed address before pounding his fist against the flimsy wood. He waited one moment, then two. There was music on inside. After knocking for the second time and receiving no answer, he twisted the knob. The door was wide open. Any predator could've barged right in. His jaw clenched, molars clamped together at the back of his mouth as he entered the apartment. Thank God it was neater than the corridors. The sounds stopped him in his tracks. A female voice singing, if you could call it that. The woman was not a songstress by any means. At the end of each verse came a belly laugh that further tightened something in his chest.

He wandered farther into the house and stopped in the living room. His throat squeezed, but not in anger, more like a wedge trying to keep a lid on the emotions bubbling to the surface. The owner of the voice danced a silly jig in front of a boy in a wheelchair, singing, twirling, stomping until he erupted in fits of laughter. Her hair was up in a messy bun, a few dark straight strands loosened around her neck. Black yoga pants and a blue tank top. A godawful voice with an alluring lilt to it. Just then, she spun and caught sight of him. Blue eyes—the color of a wide-open sky cast over the ocean—popped wide, and a shriek flew from her lips, making the kid laugh even harder. Shit, they were cute. His brother and this woman who was making the boy cackle like a hyena.

"Stay back!" He was right. There was a cadence to her voice. A hint of Scottish. Maybe Irish. The woman instantly stood before Jacob, shielding him with her frame. She wasn't short, but he wouldn't consider her tall either. Still, like most people, compared to him, she was tiny. Something akin to pride swelled in his rib cage. The fear that flashed in her eyes a moment ago was replaced by fierce protectiveness. Was this the nurse? A caregiver? "Who are you?"

"Ransom Go—" He started to say his last name, but a growl of frustration rolled over her lips. Her hands went straight to her hips.

"Ransom? That's not a real name and certainly not what you'll be doing here. Get out, or I'll…" Her voice trailed off, and her stunning eyes narrowed. She took a step forward, then another, before circling her hands around her waist.

"Hey." Without thinking, he closed the distance between them, needing to see what caused pain to flood her face. She looked a few shades paler than she had a few seconds ago. "I'm not going to hurt you."

"Not Ransom." She shook her head incredulously. "Neo Godfrey." Her gaze sliced through him, expression murderous and terrified.

What in the actual fuck?

"Wanna explain why that makes you look like you're going to vomit or execute me on the spot?"

She straightened, though she still looked as though she was going to be physically ill. "I think you should leave."

"I'm here for my brother," he ground out. "Who are

you?"

"For the first time in thirteen years." Her eyes welled, and she shook her head. "Go wait in the kitchen. I will not say what I must say to you in front of Jacob." She turned her back and went to Jacob, murmuring to him. Neo silently moved across the room.

"I'm going to turn on a movie while I talk to this person. Everything will be okay. I'll never let anyone harm you." She ran her hand over his dark hair. The action was so nurturing, so maternal a brush of envy stroked through him. Never, not once had he received the caring touch of a mother figure. He was grateful to this woman, whoever she was, for treating Jacob with tenderness. He'd known Jacob had significant medical issues, but he hadn't thought much about what that meant. His only focus had been getting to his brother. Now, standing mere feet from him, there was a pang in his heart. Life could be so unfair. He might not know Jacob, but he was still grieving for his brother. He should know the feel of his sneakers pounding on the pavement as he played with friends. Should know the freedom of crossing the room to get a toy he wanted. He was so small, muscles stiff, body leaning slightly toward the right. There was a bib around his neck and a pillow supporting his head.

"I'd never harm my own flesh and blood." He stalked forward, hands at his sides, doing his best not to look imposing, which was damn tough at six feet six inches. "Jacob." He sank to the floor beside the boy's wheelchair. He wasn't exactly sure how Jacob communicated, but he figured he'd want to be treated like anyone else his age. "I always wanted a brother, and it guts me that for the past thirteen years, I've had one who I knew nothing about. I'm so sorry. So incredibly sorry." There was a burn behind his lids, and Jacob turned his head to study him. "If I had known, I'd never have left you with our mother. I would've wanted you with me. Jacob, I'm Neo. I'm your brother."

Green eyes, so much like his own, lit with interest. Jacob studied his face, sizing him up. He could respect that. Then a smile broke over his face, and it shocked him more than an unexpected punch to the gut. The softness reflected in his brother's eyes was staggering. Fucking beautiful. With one smile, the kid welcomed him and invited him in.

So much expression in one glance, in the depths of those bottle-green eyes that communicated more than words ever could. Jacob's response encouraged him to continue. "I don't know who this lady is pulling out all the stops to make you laugh, to care for you, but I hope she knows I'm grateful." He glanced up from his crouch on the floor to find her staring at him. Another blow to the gut. His lungs were stripped of oxygen. Unlike Jacob, there was no acceptance on her face, but fuck if it wasn't the most gorgeous face he'd ever seen. For some inexplicable reason, he wanted her to want to know him, too.

"I'll speak to you in the kitchen." The woman gestured toward the hallway, and Jacob chuckled—a laugh that came from deep in his belly and made him want to grin ear to ear.

"You think it's funny when she's bossy? Or maybe it's because you know she's gonna give me an ass-kicking." More giggles. Something warm and soft spread in his chest.

She stomped into the other room, muttering about using curse words in front of a teenager.

"Okay, Jacob, be right back. Now that I know you exist, I'll always come back. Always." He stalked into the other room, noticing a pile of boxes in the hall in various stages of being shipped out. Jacob's nurse must have an online business or a side hustle of some sort. The apartment was tiny, so it didn't take long to find the proportionately small kitchen.

The woman had a kettle on the stove, and her back turned to him. He tried not to notice how well she filled out those yoga pants, but his gaze kept drawing down at all the perfection in front of him.

He cleared his throat, and she spun around. "You know my name, but I still don't know yours."

She glanced away as though contemplating how much to tell him. Working for his mother couldn't have been easy, and that alone gave him patience. "Brynn Yarrow. I've been your brother's nurse for the past five years."

"I owe you a debt that can never be repaid. When I tell you I didn't know of his existence, I swear it on everything I am. It guts me he's been displaced because of our mother's irresponsibility. That he had to move out of the manor."

Brynn tilted her head. "We were never in the manor." Her back was against the cheap laminate counter.

"Come again?" His gut twisted and he took a step closer.

She straightened, pushing her shoulders back. "We were in the carriage house."

"You're telling me that bitch put her own son outside the manor?" He clenched and unclenched his hands.

"She was constantly entertaining." Brynn tucked a strand of hair behind her ear. "Trust me when I tell you we preferred to be away from the parties and visitors. I didn't think it was safe for Jacob with people waltzing in and out at all hours of the night."

"And that's exactly the kind of statement a mother should make, yet I guarantee the thought never crossed her mind. She was never any kind of mother." No wonder Brynn looked like she'd swallowed acid when she'd placed him. Soon she'd know the kind of man he was. He may not have much capacity for emotion or warmth, but he lived by a moral code. He was a man who didn't break promises. One who was honorable. He'd have to earn her trust, and rightfully so after she'd had to work for his cold, spoiled mother. "Safe or not, it was wrong not to have you and Jacob in the house. And then the estate sells to pay her debts, and she moves you into this shithole apartment." He shook his head. They'd be out of here this evening if he had his way. "This neighborhood is not safe. The building completely unsecured. The fire detector is out of order in the corridor. Everything about this makes me sick to my stomach." Brynn's cheeks flamed, and he instantly wished he could rephrase his statement.

The expression on her face was one of shame. This couldn't be her apartment, could it? He needed to sort this cluster and fast, without insulting the angel who'd been caring for his brother. Especially if he was going to convince her to come back with him to Virginia.

CHAPTER TWO

BRYNN TURNED TO fix her tea. The steam whistling through the kettle was a blessed distraction from the shame coursing through her, no matter how she tried to shove it down. Wealthy she was not, but she'd done her best with the circumstances she'd been given. Finding an affordable apartment once Mrs. Godfrey sold the house and disappeared hadn't been easy. There were no illusions that this place was a wholesome environment for Jacob to grow up in, but she ignored that in exchange for a roof over their heads. This place was all she could afford with her savings. Paychecks had stopped months ago, but there was no way she'd leave Jacob, who was more son than patient. Now it was all for nothing because his brother was filling up the kitchen, claiming to want to be in his life. Her temples throbbed, and the urge to take Jacob and run was overwhelming.

"Brynn." For the first time since entering the apartment, Neo sounded unsure. Not once had his voice sounded uncertain since he'd stepped into the residence. Not when he'd barged in and said he was here for his brother. Not when he'd knelt down and apologized to Jacob with pain and regret radiating in his eyes. Now, though, he'd sensed her humiliation. She'd never been someone who could hide behind a poker face. "Shit. Please talk to me. Explain what's been going on."

She busied herself, reaching into the cabinet for tea bags and placing them in mugs. The kettle was heavy in her trembling hands. Fragrant steam hit the air. Lemon. Lavender. Earth. Breathe. She turned with one mug and found Neo standing right behind her. Breathing was difficult with him towering over her, filling her space and nostrils with his crisp, clean scent. His hard stare softened as he looked from the ceramic cup and then at her before surprise washed over his face. Some of the tension stiffening her shoulders ebbed. Neo had the same mother as Jacob did. That likely meant he hadn't received much care unless a nanny or other caretaker had been part of his life.

"Thank you." The appreciation in his voice as he took the mug made her heart dip. He wasn't used to being nurtured, even if it was as simple as someone making him a soothing drink. She nodded past the lump forming in her throat and brought her tea to the small table in the corner of the room. Neo followed her, pulling out the only other chair.

The warm mug heated her hands and provided a place for her to look other than Neo's face. The weight of his assessing stare made her squirm in her seat. She took a fortifying breath and prepared to tell Jacob's brother how she'd failed him in every way, starting with the unsafe neighborhood and apartment. "When the estate was sold, I had to find a place for Jacob and me."

He hissed out a breath. "Brynn, look at me."

A charged current rippled through her. Had her name ever sounded more alluring than when it was torn from

Neo's lips? She didn't think so. No, that was a lie. It hadn't. His voice was a low, rough rumble that reverberated through her body, pulsing in currents deep beneath her skin. Slowly she complied with his request, tearing her gaze away from the safety of the mug.

"You don't know me," he continued. "But you will. Wording things gently has never been a strength for me. I'm direct. To the point. More often than not, I put my foot in my mouth. I could sit here and tell you I don't make promises I might break or that I have my brother's best interests at heart. I could say I don't give the first fuck that Jacob might have big hurdles to conquer, and I want to be by his side every step of the way because you'd never believe me. But you will. Until then, all I can ask is for you to trust that I don't mean you or Jacob any harm. I know it's a big ask. You've been with my brother for five years. Five years of having someone good in his life. Of knowing someone who loves him is there. Thank you for being here when I wasn't. Kills me that I missed so goddamn much. You know him best. Please help me know him, too. Help me understand why you took on the burden of finding a place for you both to live."

She clenched her teeth to keep her chin from wobbling. This was one of those times she'd love to believe. To take the leap and trust his intentions. Jacob needed good people in his life. Ones who could see past his physical limitations to the brilliant and humorous child he was. Soak up all the love he had to give. She wanted that for him while at the same time selfishly fearing she might be cut out of Jacob's life. Still, if Jacob had the opportunity to discover a family member who'd do right by him, who was she to stop the bond from forming?

She cleared her throat. "I haven't seen or spoken to Mrs. Godfrey in over four months. When the estate was sold, she took off. We stayed in a hotel for a few nights while I tried to track her down. I never could. I knew we needed a more permanent residence, but I couldn't afford an apartment so close to the city. I hated pulling Jacob out of school, but I was so afraid he'd be put into foster care. This place was only supposed to be temporary until I could get on my feet. I've been delivering groceries. I can take Jacob with me. Also, online consignment sales have given me a boost. I'll have enough saved in a few more months to look for more secure living arrangements."

A growl rippled through the air. The man sitting across from her was fighting for calm. His jaw was set, and his lips formed a tight, thin line above his chin. "You had to deplete your savings because you haven't been getting paid. You're having to sell your stuff online? How long since you've gotten a check for Jacob's care?"

She shook her head, and a dark strand of hair slid out of its confines and settled along her cheek. "That's not what matters, right—"

"The hell it doesn't. She stopped paying you, then mailed it in when she could no longer stay in the house. It's not only gross neglect of a minor but felony child abandonment. It burns me that she died before she could answer for her crimes."

For a moment, everything stilled before a whirring filled her ears. Dead? Jacob's mother was dead. That was the reason why Neo was here. The reason he chose now to pop into his brother's life. Had he really not known about his brother? And how had he found them?

"I see questions going through your head. Ask me." Neo rested his arms on the table, leaning in closer to her.

"If you were estranged, how did you discover her death? I left her message after message with our location. I mean, she had to have written it down somewhere, yet no one tried to inform Jacob." She wrapped her hands around her mug, trying to warm her fingers despite the late summer heat.

"Two days ago, my commander and a local officer informed me of her death. Handed me a certified letter from our mother's attorney, and I called to let him know I had no interest in anything she left in her will. He told me that she'd been in significant debt and nothing of monetary value had been left to my brother or me. Her death wasn't surprising. Ever since I was a kid, she lived hard and reckless. It was the news that I had a brother that knocked me on my ass. I'm sorry you didn't know."

"Are you in the military?" She took a sip of the tea. The strong, warm flavors usually soothed her. Not today.

"Yes." He sat up straighter, studying her.

"What branch?" She set down her tea and clasped her hands together to keep them from shaking. She didn't want to lose Jacob.

"Navy. We're going to be deploying soon. I want to ensure all the necessary custody paperwork has been pushed through before I leave and Jacob is added to my benefits."

"Is that why you introduced yourself as Ransom? Is that some kind of nickname?" If she kept asking him questions, it would delay asking what she really needed to know. How far he was taking Jacob out of her life.

"Yes. That's what I was coined during training. It stuck."

"Why Ransom? Did you save a whole slew of hostages?" She rotated the mug in her hands.

He lifted the tea to his lips and took a sip. "There's absolutely nothing heroic behind it, unfortunately. There was a guy who snuck off base to see his girlfriend. I saw him sneaking back in and he begged me not to say anything. Was scared to death of being quarter-decked."

Brynn raised a brow.

"Oh, that's when you have to do an insane amount of exercise under the scrutiny of a drill instructor. The guy offered to keep me supplied with chocolate chip cookies once we could start receiving packages. His mom owned a bakery and I have a sweet tooth. Everyone joked that I demanded his mom's cookies as ransom."

Okay, enough stalling. "Where is your base?" She closed her eyes for a moment, not wanting him to see her expression when he announced his location if it ended up being halfway around the country.

"Virginia."

The location of his base could be so much worse. She was thankful, even if it would be a hike to visit Jacob.

The urge to sink to the floor and wallow was overwhelming. Everything was happening so fast. How had such an ordinary day deteriorated so quickly? Neo had burst through their door and threatened to leave with everything she loved. Her eyelids burned, and she swiped away the first hot tear before it could hit her cheek. She buried her face into the oversized tea mug as though it would somehow help conceal her emotions from Jacob's brother. She inhaled slowly, then released the breath. The questions she had might be hard, but she wouldn't let Neo leave with his brother without an understanding of what his care was going to be like on a daily basis.

"How do you plan to care for Jacob when you're deployed? He needs total assistance."

He was quiet for a moment, those sea-glass-green eyes studying, assessing. "Do you have family in the area?"

She shook her head and straightened her shoulders. "I was born in Ireland but came to America with my grandmother when I was a teenager. She passed on my eighteenth birthday." A shiver raced down her spine. Every so often, she'd wake up with a scream caught in her throat, the sheets tangled like manacles around her ankles, and sweat seeping from her pores. The incidents that led her to America were no longer part of her life. A locked door that remained deadbolted and sealed off.

"Damn. I'm sorry."

"It was a long time ago." That was the truth, but she still pined for the scent of fresh dough and floured countertops. She missed walking along the shoreline and collecting shells. Of lavender peppered hugs and baskets of yarn by the couch.

He stared at her a moment longer. "To answer your question, I intend to care for Jacob by giving him everything he needs to thrive. An easily accessible environment—a one-story home, or I can get us a condo for the time being. If it doesn't have the necessary ramps, my team and I can build them. I'm going to get him enrolled in school. Hire a fantastic nurse."

God, that hurt.

"Brynn." He waited until she met his gaze. "I mean you. I want you to come to Virginia with us if you're willing. I'll do whatever it takes to make sure Jacob has what he needs, but you're right—I don't know what he requires and I'm not exactly what you'd call nurturing, although I'll try. I need you to guide me. I'll cover your relocation costs and double whatever my mother was paying you—starting with the months she still owes you."

"I'd never ask you to—"

"Didn't have to, sweetheart." There was a pang in her heart. No one had ever called her that before. "A lesser person would've buckled under the financial pressure our mother put you under. That stops now. Listen, I know what I'm asking is too much. Know it's unfair, but I'm selfish. I need your insight, but more than that, Jacob needs you. There's love there. I see that. Something I would never want to tear apart. Sleep on it. Please."

"I don't need to sleep on it. Jacob's the only family I have, and he's like a son to me. I'll go where he goes and help you with what you need."

"Thank fuck. I'll never leave you to struggle like my mother did. You have no idea how grateful I am. What are the chances I can convince you to come back to the hotel with me?"

He must've caught her disapproving look because he cleared his throat and continued. "I'll reserve additional rooms. I'd feel better if you both had a safe place to stay the night. And that's not me trying to be a dick and say this place isn't good enough. It's not safe. That simple."

"Jacob's medical equipment is here."

"I can move it. Anything you need, I'll load up. I can come back and pick up anything that can wait for the morning."

God, how she wanted to get out of here. She hadn't slept a whole night since they came to the apartment. The couple above them was constantly screaming, fighting. The police had been called more than once. Mostly by her. The locks were so flimsy that she'd installed a dead bolt of her own. She glanced at the man across from her. Good looks could be deceptive, but his words weren't sugarcoated. He was rough and raw. For some reason, she trusted him more because of it. She looked away, and her cheeks heated. Her sensitive skin, quick to redden when embarrassed or angry, always gave her away.

"I wanna know what turned your cheeks that shade." His voice was so low that she would've missed what he said if they weren't sitting so close to one another.

Never in a million years. "It's warm in here." And it was. The summer months had been stifling without air conditioning in the building. She'd purchased a small air conditioner for Jacob's room, but it only did so much. Still, the weather wasn't the reason her cheeks were on fire. Not recognizing this man's broad chest and sculpted arms was impossible. His face was equally masculine, with a defined jawline and high cheeks. And good grief, she had no reason to look at Jacob's brother like he was a delicious treat. Especially not if he was going to be her employer.

"All the more reason to come with me to the hotel."

"Okay." Her lips moved before her brain caught up to what she'd agreed to. "If they have availability, we'll come with you." The contents of her life could be thrown into an oversized garbage bag. The drab couch had come with the apartment, and she'd been sleeping on it to give Jacob the bed. She'd been going through the motions since Jacob's mother had run off, her gut a twisted knot, exhaustion riding her hard. Maybe this was the fresh start they needed, and while she was still skeptical of Neo, for the first time in a long time, there was hope.

CHAPTER THREE

BY THE TIME they made it up to their hotel rooms, Neo had an additional layer of respect for Brynn. When he'd loaded up the medical equipment into Brynn's run-down van, she patiently explained what each device was for and how often his brother needed it. She'd taught him how lower the accessible ramp on her vehicle, which was in desperate need of updating, and secure Jacob's wheelchair. Brynn had explained how his brother used total-body communication to interact, but he hadn't fully understood until he'd observed how she fluidly modified her questions so he could answer with a turn of his head or give one of those brilliant smiles. She made it all look so easy, when it was anything but.

He wanted to do the right thing. To be the man his father never was. To nurture like his mother hadn't. Watching Brynn, though, with her tender disposition, rocked him back. Honor, courage, and control were qualities he had in spades. Wasn't sure if he had it in him to truly love, to offer soft words, to develop an emotional connection with anyone outside his team. Shae Godfrey had planted her poisonous words and indifference so goddamn deep, he wasn't sure he'd ever be able to extract all of the self-doubt and hurt.

Following Brynn's lead would help. He'd been prepared

to beg and bribe Brynn to relocate to Virginia, but the bond she had with Jacob wouldn't allow for anything else. He wanted to ask her more about her life in Ireland and her childhood, but she was on overload as it was. Still, she hadn't mentioned a thing about her parents. Maybe her childhood was similar to his, with the only guiding caretaker a grandparent. Now they were up in Jacob's room, which was adjacent to his. She insisted she was fine bunking with Jacob, but after months in that shoebox apartment, he wanted her to have a little space to herself. The connecting door would allow her to check in on Jacob during the night if there was a need.

"OH, NO." BRYNN'S brows shot up as she looked at the card she'd drawn from the deck. "I've been sued to the tune of one hundred thousand. Seems a bit steep."

"Fork it over." He growled, and Jacob chuckled. For some reason, his brother seemed to find his brusque tone hilarious. They were all sitting on his brother's king bed, playing the Game of Life. At first, he'd been extremely uncomfortable playing the board game. He was out of his element and still wasn't quite sure how to interact with his brother. Learning how to communicate with Jacob was a given, but he'd never been around someone who was non-verbal before, or with so many medical challenges. He didn't want to screw things up or say the wrong thing. Brynn seamlessly interpreted his expressions and movements. Right now, it seemed impossible to achieve that level of fluid communication during his two-week emergency leave.

Jacob was propped into a sitting position in a sea of pillows, Brynn had her legs crossed beneath her on one side of the bed, and he was lying on his side opposite her with the board game in the middle. On a dramatic sigh, she counted out the colorful bills and passed them over. Her pinkie finger slid against his palm, and the urge to grab her hand and hold it in his was overwhelming. She was anchoring him. Making all the hurdles that lay ahead seem possible. Their eyes met and held. Before long a rosy hue was rising up her delicate cheekbones, which brought him back to the moment in her apartment when her face had suddenly gone ablaze. Had she been thinking of him? Of some inappropriate vision that popped into her head? His skin tingled. There was no denying she was stunning. The combination of black velvet hair and cobalt eyes was arresting. Add in the mix of sweet determination that he'd witnessed from her in the past few hours and he was damn impressed.

"All right, you're up, Jacob." Brynn held up one of his brother's hands and put the dice in his palm. "Tell me when you're ready to roll." His brother let out a sound that was between a whoop and a delighted cry, casting his beautiful stare in Brynn's direction. Just because his brother didn't articulate with words didn't mean he couldn't communicate. He used his smile, his eyes, a turn of his head to share what was on his mind. Brynn shook Jacob's hand and helped him toss the dice on the bed. "Ten spots. Good roll." She counted out the spaces and inched Jacob's car forward. "Ah, of course the legendary luck continues. You've hit payday."

What could only be described as a satisfied smirk quirked

his brother's cheek. "How much does a secret agent make again?" Neo asked about Jacob's choice of careers.

"Seventy-five thousand." Brynn collected the rogue dice off the comforter. Since they'd walked into the lobby of the hotel, Brynn's whole demeanor had relaxed. It was clear she'd been worried sick over Jacob, her finances, and their living conditions. Still, she'd pushed forward. He was more than happy to step in and shoulder some of the weight. They were now both of his responsibility. He wasn't sure if Brynn even knew how much he needed her right now.

He counted out the money from the bank and placed it in Jacob's pile, which was rapidly expanding. He did seem to have a stroke of luck with this game. They played for another hour, and when they tallied up their money after repaying their loans, Jacob came out on top. The kid looked very pleased with himself. He couldn't remember the last time he'd had such an enjoyable night or a time when he sat down and played a game other than cards with his teammates, and even that was rare.

"All right, Jacob, it's way past your bedtime." Brynn stretched, raising her hands above her head. The position accentuated the curve of her breasts pressing against her tank top. She caught him staring, and she quickly lowered her arms.

Great. Just what she wanted. Someone leering at her. Fucking this up, scaring her off would leave him and Jacob completely vulnerable. Trust didn't come easy for him, and it would be difficult to hand his brother's care over to someone who didn't know him well. "What's the nighttime routine?" he said to push past the awkward moment.

She cleared her throat, and uncrossed her legs to slide off of the bed. "Some daily living activities like getting cleaned up and brushing his teeth. He takes several medications—anticonvulsants, muscle relaxers, and ones to prevent seizures. The dressings around his G-tube, that's a port that delivers additional food directly to his stomach, needs to be changed. Overnight, he gets supplemental nutrition via tube. We get into pajamas, and set up his breathing treatments so they're running while we read a chapter of whatever book we have."

"Jesus." He glanced at his brother, then at Brynn, and back. "I'm sorry. Sorry you have to deal with all this extra shit. You must be one hell of a brave kid." Jacob offered no response, but the thoughtful look on his face indicated he was listening to each word.

"He is." Brynn nodded and walked to the top of the bed, sitting at the side next to Jacob. "And resilient. Isn't that right, Jacob? I'm going to talk about you for a minute." She ran her hand over his hair. He liked that Brynn always told his brother what was happening. It must be hard to have people talk about you like you weren't in the room, just because you couldn't communicate in the same way. "But the thing is, despite what Jacob deals with on a day-to-day basis, your brother has so much joy. So much love he shares with his friends and teachers. With me. There are so many things he loves, too—books, the water, playing board games, and watching fish at the aquarium. And the way he brings people together with that deep belly laugh is amazing. In his old school, he played on several unified sports teams. Was very involved in the community. I'm hoping once we get settled in Virginia we can find programs and groups for him to belong to. What I'm trying to say is some people go through their whole life without knowing the kind of love, support, and joy that Jacob does."

Something hard had wedged itself into the base of his throat, and he couldn't seem to find words to share how beautiful he thought Brynn's perspective was.

As if sensing his discomfort, Brynn cleared her throat. "Now speaking of books, that reminds me, I need to return the one we have to the library before we go anywhere." Her expression was pinched. He shook his head, suppressing a grin. Goddamn adorable that she'd be so concerned about returning a book with everything else she had going on.

"Okay. We'll return the book first thing," he reassured her. His pocket vibrated against his leg with an incoming call. He fished the phone out of his pocket and glanced at the screen. It was Joker.

"Go take your call. We'll see you in the morning." Brynn was already unpacking a change of clothes from Jacob's suitcase.

The bed creaked as he stood. "I was hoping to talk to you before you go to sleep." He swiped his finger across the screen to silence the call.

Brynn hesitated, almost drawing back into herself. And of course she did. They'd just met. She'd taken a big risk by coming to the hotel, and he was pushing her beyond her comfort zone. He had questions about logistics. When it was feasible for her to consider leaving Boston and what needed to be prepared when they arrived in Virginia, but she didn't know his intentions. When his team had discovered Jacob's location, he'd arranged to meet his mother's lawyer, and he'd hired one of his own to ensure Jacob's best interests. She laid the pajamas on the end of the bed, then opened a bag containing a half dozen medications, before turning to him. "It's late. You can ask me now or we can talk tomorrow."

Telling her she was safe with him wasn't going to ease her mind. He needed to gain her trust and Jacob's. He nodded. "Tomorrow I have a meeting with the lawyer who is handling our mother's estate, including the guardianship of Jacob. I've hired my own lawyer to be in attendance."

"What time?" Her shoulders relaxed a fraction, but she still glanced over her shoulder with a wary expression when she turned her back to gather more supplies from her bag. Again, he couldn't blame her for being smart, even as his stomach turned at the thought of her being afraid of him. He took a few steps back, moving closer toward the door.

"The firm sent me an email that they've had a cancellation tomorrow morning at eight o'clock, but if that's too soon, we can keep the first appointment I made for two days from now." His palm hit the cool metal door handle. The more space he gave Brynn, the more she seemed to relax. That didn't sit well with him. Anger combusted and seared through his chest. Someone had mistreated her. His intuition was rarely off, but damn, he hoped he was wrong.

"Tomorrow's fine." Brynn stood near the side of the bed fidgeting with the plastic bag of supplies in her hands. "I'll have Jacob ready."

He felt like he should ask if there was anything he could help with in the morning, but didn't know if he'd be overstepping.

"Thank you." He held her gaze for a moment, wanting to thank her again, but not wanting to make her uncomfortable. "Night, Jacob. I had fun with you. Can't wait for you to meet my teammates. They'll be your brothers, too." Jacob looked up at him in acknowledgment. His brother's eyes were getting heavy, but he was offered a sleepy smile. His heart did a funny squeeze as he stepped into the hall and crossed to his room to call Joker back.

His friend answered on the first ring. "Where the hell have you been the last two hours?"

Joker had an intense and serious personality—part of the reason he earned his nickname. "Playing the Game of Life with my brother and his nurse at the hotel we're staying in." He rolled his tight shoulders. The day had been intense between meeting his brother and trying to convince Brynn he meant no harm.

"When Silver told me you found them and convinced them to go with you I didn't believe it. Be careful, man. You don't know this woman. She could be looking for a payday." Joker was also extremely wary of people. He'd grown up in the Alaskan bush with his twin sister and their father. Their mother had left when they were both young.

"That's exactly what she's going to get." He removed his room key from his wallet, scanned it, and pushed the door open. Conditioned air swept over him as he made his way into the room. "My mother stopped paying her four months ago. Four fucking months, Joker. You should've seen where they were living. And before then, they lived on the grounds of my mother's estate—not in it." He went straight for the minibar and removed a beer.

"Seriously jacked. But then again, are you surprised?" Joker asked vehemently. He might be moody and distrusting, but his loyalty to those he loved was fierce and profound.

"No. Just disgusted. I thought fucking up one kid would be enough for her. She must've gotten knocked up a couple years after I left. Probably around the time we were finishing BUD/S. I just keep thinking if I'd gone back, even once, I would've found out about Jacob." He sank back onto the crisp white comforter covering the bed, feet still planted on the floor.

"Don't do that. You could've, but you didn't. What's your next move?" Joker was never one for softening words. He held the cell phone between his jaw and his shoulder, and using the bottle opener on his keychain, popped the top off of his drink. Barley-scented vapor from the chilled bottle rose into the air. "Sad as it is, it only took Brynn an hour to pack up, and most of the possessions were Jacob's. His medical equipment took up most of the space. She only had one garbage bag of belongings."

"That set off any red flags for you?" Joker asked.

He did wonder how it was possible she had so little in the way of belongings, She sold her own things to support herself and his brother. If that didn't say something about her character, he wasn't sure what did. "I don't think there's anything suspicious about her if that's what you're asking. In fact, she's a fucking angel."

"So it's like that." There was a rare teasing note in Joker's voice.

"It's not like anything. She's amazing with Jacob. Loves

him like a mother. What she does for him on a daily basis blows my mind, and she makes it look easy. Having her come back to Virginia just makes everything that much more manageable. When we go out on missions, my mind will be at peace because I know she'd never let anything harm Jacob." And if any one of his teammates tried to hook up with her like she was some woman they'd pick up at the bar, they had another think coming. An ugly burn roiled in his stomach. It wasn't jealousy. He was feeling protective of her because she was important to Jacob.

"What do you need us to do? Doubt the commander will let you sit out on this next mission." The next mission wasn't an if, but a when. They were standing by for their CIA source to confirm reports of a key militant's location. A new terrorist group had splintered off from the Islamic State – Khorasan Province and swelled in numbers when the United States withdrew from Afghanistan. The group was responsible for the malicious deaths of thousands of women and children, and intel suggested they'd have the means to carry out an attack on US soil within six months.

"Search some listings for me. A single family home—a ranch, or a condo unit with elevator access. The closer to base and the public middle school the better. Also, car dealerships in the area that sell accessible vans." A dull throb began to pulse behind his eyes. The sheer number of things he needed to do to get Jacob settled in Virginia pressed heavily on his shoulders. Still, he wasn't going to turn on his heel and walk out in the face of responsibility like his dad or just plain ignore it like his mother. Jacob was his blood, and he'd planned to do right by him.

"The commander's nephew is a real estate agent. I'll get in touch. I'll need to do some digging on the vehicle."

"Appreciate it."

When they disconnected, he glanced at the time on his phone. Nine o'clock. After everything Brynn had been through the last few months, she needed rest. If there was something he could do to ease some of her stress, he'd do it in a heartbeat, but he didn't want to overstep or scare her. Not that he had the first idea how to care for Jacob's needs yet, but he'd learn. That she'd stay with Jacob after repeatedly not getting paid said a lot about her as a person and just how much Jacob meant to her. Maybe he didn't know some of the other details about his brother's nurse, but what he'd seen impressed the hell out of him. He didn't trust easily, and after enduring dangerous missions he was most secure when he was in control. Having faith in another person outside his team usually left the fine hairs on the back of his neck standing up and his heart beating out of his chest, and in this situation he really was a fish out of water. Needing someone was a completely new experience, but he was lucky it was Brynn. The respect was there already, and if he made a mistake, she'd call him on it. Now, he just needed to figure out how to be a good brother, make the legal guardianship of Jacob official, find a living space that would meet everyone's needs, and put a dozen other things in motion so his brother would have everything he needed. Despite the stress of his two-week timeframe, he was looking forward to getting to know his brother better. Being a positive role model in Jacob's life was a mission he refused to fail.

CHAPTER FOUR

MONEY SPOKE. OR ties to a family with old money did. That was Brynn's takeaway from their meeting at the lawyer's office as they stepped from the opulent building and into the rainy New England day. Jacob's mother might've squandered her inheritance, but between the fancy hotel they were staying in and how appointments just happened to become available for him, she was beginning to realize he'd probably been a bit smarter about his money than his mother. Neo having money didn't necessarily bother her—it meant that Jacob would be supported and she would get paid—but it did feel as though they were on very different playing fields. She gripped the handles of Jacob's wheelchair more tightly. She didn't like having someone else's power held over her, and sometimes she forgot that not everyone would use their status or wealth to sway others. Right now, she was glad for the sounds of the city, because her bare feet were currently squelching inside her sneakers with every puddle she couldn't dodge.

Neo slowed as they neared a crosswalk and hit the pedestrian button. They waited silently as thick droplets slid into her hair, prickling her scalp and making her shiver. For summer, it was a brisk day, and they were close to Boston Harbor. She'd refused Neo's jacket. He'd even taken it off and insisted she wear it, but she wouldn't put it on. Accepting lodging and food before she was officially under his employment didn't sit well with her, but leaving Jacob and going back to the apartment wasn't an option. Taking the jacket off of Neo's back when it was pouring wasn't going to happen. The pedestrian walk sign began to flash, and Neo stepped out onto the street first, scanning the road before helping her guide the wheelchair over the slight ridge of the sloped curb. Jacob was bundled beneath his own rain jacket. The green material billowed around his chair, keeping him nice and warm.

"Where are we going?" They had walked in the direction of the parking garage, but instead, he turned toward a storefront and pulled open the glass door.

"We need to stop in here." Neo held open the door and waited expectantly. A trio of business professionals walked briskly down the sidewalk, skirting around her and Jacob. Moving out of their way would've been the nice thing to do, but her feet were glued to the pavement.

"In a women's boutique?" Her heartbeat quickened.

"Please come out of the rain." There was a pleading note in his eyes that made her step forward, sliding Jacob's wheelchair onto the tile floor. Beads of water from his cloak and her soaked shoes left little puddles on the floor.

"Look, we're making a mess." She gestured at the floor around her feet. "Someone might slip, and—"

"Oh, don't worry about it." Brynn hadn't noticed the salesperson approaching with a rolled-up mat. "I should've put this thing out hours ago." She offered a bright, carefree smile. Her face was unlined and unblemished, maybe a college student from one of the many universities in the city. "What are you coming in for today?"

"Nothing." Her voice was clipped, and she instantly regretted her tone when the girl's expression wavered with confusion.

"Everything," Neo said in an equally strong voice. "My friend needs some essentials." The girl's gaze went from her to Neo and back again.

She raised her chin. "If you have a need for a skirt or lacy panties, go ahead and take your time. Jacob and I will be here."

"How about I give you two a minute?" The girl flashed her an apologetic grin and scurried toward the register.

Her ribs were tight, making it difficult to fill her lungs. "If you're here to buy yourself or a girlfriend something, fine. But if you're thinking of buying me clothes as some sort of charity, I don't need them." She skirted around to the front of Jacob's chair. "I need a minute to discuss something with your brother. We're going to step to the side, but we'll be here." She searched her phone for music by one of Jacob's favorite artists, left the phone in the travel bag attached to the wheelchair, and ushered Neo a few feet away.

The moment they were far enough from Jacob, Neo started laying in. "My mother failed to pay you for months. You sold your things to provide for Jacob. Please, let me replace some of the necessary items you've gotten rid of to help support my brother. This is not charity. Not even close." Neo stood solidly, feet planted wide. He was a man used to getting his way.

"I'm not comfortable with that." She tried to mirror his

strong stance. "If I buy something, it's going to be with my money. The feeling of being indebted to you is not how I want to begin this working relationship."

His expression softened. "That's just it," he said, taking a step closer. "Right now, I'm indebted to you. There are things you absolutely need. I know you prepared for the day and researched the weather because you have my brother bundled in his raincoat, hat, and sweatshirt. You're wearing a T-shirt, jeans, and shoes that have breaks in the material. You packed your belongings in one bag. I'm not saying this to put you down. Please don't take it that way. I just want you to be comfortable, and that means having the basics you need to protect you from the elements."

"The equity between us is more important to me than material things. Let's stop this silliness and get back to the hotel. I imagine there are still many loose strings to tie up before the move to Virginia." Brynn started to turn, ready to take Jacob and go back into the rain. The prominent goose bumps up and down her arms weren't helping her argument. She was cold and wet, but soon she'd have a steady paycheck and buy a new pair of sneakers and some sweatshirts. Being uncomfortable for one day was nothing in the grand scheme of things.

"So, it doesn't sound like trust or help comes easy for either of us." Neo's low words stopped her. "But I'm not trying to give you things so you feel indebted to me. I'm investing in the most important healthcare professional in Jacob's life. If you don't have what you need, if you get trench foot from walking through the rain or sick because you're forgoing food to pay for things my brother needs, there'll be no one to take care of Jacob." He sighed and raked his hands through his hair. "Don't you realize that I need you more than you need anything I could offer you? That's hard as fuck for me to accept. Needing someone. You having more control than I do. If anything, you hold the power in this relationship, Brynn. Not me. If it makes you feel better, I'll deduct the cost of the clothes from the four months' pay my mother failed to provide."

Her resolve wavered for the first time. He really wanted to do what was right. Maybe it was his military training or maybe he just had a high code of honor, but he was determined to carry out his mission. Neo might not see it that way, but she suspected that's how he thought of them—that it was his duty to care for Jacob, and in turn, her as well. "I don't want you to be responsible for your mother's debt. I'm happy to have a steady job and be with Jacob, okay?"

He squinted slightly, eyes lit with amusement. "Shit you're stubborn." A ghost of a smile flitted across his lips.

"Better that you get used to it now." Thank God her voice stayed steady when she was feeling anything but. She was trying not to notice how his eyes crinkled at the corners or the slightly mischievous smirk on his face.

He cleared his throat and schooled his expression. "Right, well, can we make some kind of deal here?"

Finally, they were getting somewhere. "We start fresh. You let go of the guilt of your mother not paying me and I'll accept a few items."

He put his hands on his hips. "Three months' pay, clothes and shoes, plus I get to take you and Jacob to the aquarium after this."

She contemplated for a moment, letting the silence hang in the space between them. "Two months, under three hundred dollars' worth of items, and the aquarium, because Jacob loves it."

"Damn, woman. You could have a career as a lawyer or an arbitrator. Fine." He held out his hand, and Brynn shook it, quickly letting go when a spark tingled up her arm.

The salesperson chose that exact moment to come back, a smile on her face, and hands clasped in anticipation. "Are you ready to go take a look? I can help you choose, if shopping isn't your thing."

"Please, Brynn. Go. Take your time. Jacob and I can catch up on the baseball game."

She sighed and rubbed her temple. "I won't be long."

Forty-five minutes later, Brynn was leaving the store with a new pair of jeans, a couple of shirts, a windbreaker, and a sturdy pair of sneakers. Neo held up his end of the deal and didn't push her to get more. She was secretly thrilled by the feel of the new shoes, and the buttery, stretchy fabric of the jeans. The only uncomfortable moment was when the salesperson tried to get her to try on shorts, but she respected Brynn's wishes when she adamantly refused. She was self-conscious about her scars, and that was something that wouldn't change, even if summer did get a bit hot with fabric hugging her from hip to ankle.

The red-brick path toward the aquarium was one she and Jacob had walked many times. Jacob's head was turning from left to right, taking in the sights. Less than ten feet from them, a trio of seagulls spread their wings and swooped to the ground for a discarded cracker, squabbling over their find. In the distance, the harbor churned, dark and choppy, with tiny waves cresting with whitecaps. Before his mom left, Brynn would spend hours walking with Jacob around Boston Harbor and visiting the aquarium. She was glad they were able to visit again before they left for Virginia.

A gust of wind tangled through her hair, carrying a spray of ocean mist. She coated her lungs with salt and brine-laden air. "I don't want to admit it, but I'm much more comfortable now that I have this jacket. Thank you." It wasn't lost on her that for the first time, she'd trusted someone besides her beloved grandmother, a man, without some terrible repercussion following. Without strings or pain.

"I don't want gratitude." His expression shuttered. "Not to mention you bought every piece."

The hood of Jacob's coat blew forward, covering his eyes, and she smoothed it back. "You're not going to say I told you so?" She stole a glance at him, but he was already looking down at her intently.

"No." His jaw was hard and well defined. At first, he appeared cold with no softness to be found, especially in the sea-glass-green depths of his eyes. She wasn't afraid of him, though. All the subtle nuances of his body language screamed protector. The way he was constantly assessing their surroundings or stepping off of the curb first, then turning his body toward her and Jacob like he was creating a physical barrier between them and traffic. He swore. He was blunt. But she knew better than most that evil sometimes lived beneath smooth, polished surfaces. "I will never say I told you so. Your choices are your own, and I'm sure you have good reason for making them."

There was no line at the outdoor ticket counter, a stark contrast to weekend days during the summer. Neo purchased admission for three, and they paused to watch the seals sliding and weaving in the water through an outdoor viewing center. When they entered, there was a green screen set up in the corner of the lobby with a photographer, just beyond the turnstiles. One of the aquarium employees directed them to an accessible gate and ushered them through.

"Welcome to the New England Aquarium. Step right over here so we can get a family photo for you." The man holding the camera grinned. She paused, waiting for Neo to correct the man but he didn't.

She took a few steps to the right and crouched beside the front wheels of Jacob's chair. "Would you like a picture with your brother?" She gave him the option of yes or no. He chose yes.

Neo stepped closer. "Should we get Brynn in this picture, too?" Jacob immediately turned his head toward his brother.

"I guess we're all taking a photo, then." She didn't do social media—a bunch of photographs of her circulating around the internet didn't sit well. Not that she was hiding, but she was cautious. This was different, though; it was just one picture. The camera man could've played the role of Santa Claus during the winter months, but each time he lowered his camera, the twinkle in his eye was only visible through the glaze of his tears.

The photographer removed the camera strap from his neck and put down his equipment. "Would it be okay for me to say hello?" The man's voice was thick with emotion.

Neo tensed beside her. Without thinking, she gave his arm a gentle squeeze of reassurance. His muscles bunched beneath her touch, and he froze. She dropped her hand at his reaction. Shoot. Neo's body language told her loud and clear that he didn't appreciate being touched, and even though she had the most innocent of intentions, she'd crossed a hard line. Pushing the awkward moment with Neo to the back of her mind, she took a few steps forward. "Jacob enjoys meeting new people." Brynn gave the older man an encouraging smile.

"My granddaughter, Rose, is at Boston Children's Hospital." The man shuffled closer. "She was recently diagnosed with cerebral palsy. They say she's going to be nonambulatory." The man painstakingly lowered himself down to one knee and moved his gaze from Brynn to Jacob. "Hi there." He stopped to clear his throat. "I'm Bill. My granddaughter's going to be getting a pair of wheels like this soon."

Jacob looked at him and offered one of his blinding smiles, and his eyes shined with so much light it was like clouds parting, soaking everything in sunshine. The man's eyes filled. "It's helped me to meet you. Your road can't be easy, but your smile…it helps me, you know. Seeing you look so happy with your family here, it helps. You must be one tough kid." He patted Jacob's arm and slowly rose on slightly bowed legs.

A tight knot formed in Brynn's throat, and she moved forward, wrapping her arms around the old man's neck. "And Rose will help others someday, too. The diagnosis is hard, but your family isn't alone. Children with medical challenges might have different obstacles, more challenges, but I've learned through my time with Jacob that they're resilient and determined. Their lives can be filled with happiness and joy like anyone else. I'd like to give you my email address if that's okay, in case your family wants to connect."

The man drew his hands across his cheek, brushing off the tears. He mouthed *thank you* and walked back to the desk positioned in front of the green screen, picking up a pamphlet for the aquarium. She grabbed a pen from the table and noted down her contact information before their trio entered the building at the penguin habitat. While she and Jacob watched the flightless birds dive and dip through the water, she could feel Neo's eyes on her. And when they ascended the walkway that wound around a giant ocean tank, she was sure his gaze was more focused on her than the shimmering scales gliding through the coral reef.

Neo's intensity unnerved her. Made her brain unfocused and her hands and feet clumsy. Maybe he was still wondering why she'd touched his arm, but her knee-jerk reaction had been to soothe some of the distress that was rolling off of him. She wouldn't make the same mistake twice. She wasn't sure what he was looking for or whether he'd eventually find it, and she certainly shouldn't care beyond his perception of her nursing abilities. Shouldn't and wouldn't. They were nothing but an employer and an employee.

CHAPTER FIVE

NEO LEANED BACK in the ergonomic chair, trying and failing to get Jacob's nurse off of his mind. Brynn's goodness once again put him to shame. Although a flare of protectiveness swept over him when she gave out her personal information, he couldn't deny that she'd touched the photographer at the aquarium. Bottom line, if the world had more Brynns it would be a hell of a nicer place. When the photographer asked to say hello to Jacob, he'd been hit with a wave of stress, unsure of the man's intentions. Then, the weight of Brynn's small hand had landed on his elbow, letting him know it was all right. Her touch had instantly settled something inside him. It was natural. Right. So much so that his body instantly fired off warning signals. She could mean something to him. Maybe she already did. Staying solidly in place, barely breathing, was the only way to rein in the powerful sensation coursing through him. Vulnerability laced with anticipation. The sense that he'd stumbled upon a treasure. One that if he was smart, he'd die to keep.

Of course, that line of thinking was absurd. He'd never let a woman close enough to own his heart. Any hint of an emotional connection and he was out the door—not that he'd ever felt something for a woman beyond physical attraction. Brynn was different. He could already feel her taking root beneath his skin, and his brain sure as hell didn't want her there, but his heart hadn't gotten the message. A therapist would say he had issues of self-worth and rejection. They wouldn't be wrong. Blocks of small hurts had stacked up one after the other, until his emotions were sealed off behind the impenetrable wall they'd constructed.

Still, when they got back to the hotel, he'd watched Brynn administer Jacob's medications and treatments, trying his best to keep up, and he'd been impressed. She was so swift and efficient. Movements brisk and calculated, yet warm and tender. He'd met Jacob and Brynn in the lobby restaurant for dinner, and was surprised when she told him she was ready to discuss their relocation to Virginia after Jacob was tucked in for the night. The previous night, she was wary to have him in the same space as her, but now she'd invited him in. A little part of her trusted him, and that felt damn good. He glanced at the time on his cell phone and stood from the workspace in the corner of the hotel room. On a whim, he grabbed two small bottles of wine and another beer from the mini fridge, in case that's what she preferred, and crossed the hall.

He lifted his hand and rapped quietly on the door. It swung open, and for what seemed like the hundredth time that day her eyes, so blue, connected with his, stealing the breath from his lungs. Her hair was damp, the dark strands spilling over her white, robe-clad shoulders.

"Did you check the peephole before you opened the door?" His voice was harsher than he intended. When it came to safety, it was in his nature to notice the danger in every crevice of his surroundings.

"Of course I did." She frowned at him and retreated back to let him inside.

"Good. You never know." The door shut behind him.

"You certainly don't." She was glancing down at her hands when he turned to wait for her. He didn't want to assume she was okay with him making himself at home in her space.

"Personal experience?" As soon as he said the words, his gut clenched. What if it was? If she'd been hurt? He already knew she didn't like to depend on anyone but herself, was proud, and was reluctant to trust. He hated to think there was a specific person or event that had made her wary of others.

"Common sense." Her face revealed nothing, but a shadow darkened her eyes. Only for a moment, but it was there all the same. He wasn't going to pressure her into discussing something she didn't want to. At least not tonight.

"I know you have your own minibar, but I brought these over. Wasn't sure what you liked." He hesitated. Maybe she didn't drink at all. Questioning himself was something new, and it had everything to do with the woman standing in front of him in slipper-clad feet. Her presence made the floor tilt beneath his feet.

"Thank you." She picked the white wine from his hand and carried it to the bureau, pouring the contents into one of the glasses near the coffee maker. "Jacob loved that giant stuffed penguin you got him at the aquarium, and the photographs."

She didn't know that he'd taken one of the pictures from the aquarium, too, and slid it into his wallet. Today was one of the best days he'd had in a long time, and he wanted to keep the memory. The bond he had with Jacob was growing stronger, and even though he still doubted his ability to provide care without Brynn, signing the guardianship paperwork today felt less like a duty he'd sworn to see through and more like the foundation of something beautiful. Something wholesome. He was scared to death.

"But…" Brynn continued, her voice taking on an accusatory tone. "You didn't stick to the deal we made in the store."

The sudden urge to kiss the determined frown off of her lips was so strong, it took him aback. Fuck. He had to keep things professional. Brynn took her drink to the love seat by the window and sat, tucking her feet beneath her. She took up so little space curled up, he sat on the other side of the couch instead of in the desk chair like he'd planned.

"How so?" Maybe he'd snuck in a few extra clothing items from the aquarium, and the seahorse, because when she watched them, her eyes had glowed with an ethereal wonder he wouldn't soon forget. The stuffed animal was probably juvenile. Maybe she'd throw it in the back of her closet. The idea of her snuggling into bed with something he'd bought, gaining comfort from it, won out his internal tug-of-war and he found himself carrying it to the register.

"You don't need to ask me that. If you think you managed to slip it past me, you're wrong. The bag you gave me after dinner tonight—the sweatshirts. The stuffed animal. You found a loophole in our deal and exploited it to the fullest."

Goddamn. That pout on her lips. Adorable. "I wouldn't

say to the fullest. I could've loaded up a shit ton more, but I figured you'd get sick of hoodies with mermaids and sea creatures." The mermaid on one of the sweatshirts had caught his eye. If the mythical sirens were real, he'd imagine they'd look like Brynn with her dark hair and big eyes. "They're just a couple of souvenirs. You're doing something profound for me. Makes me want to spoil you a bit."

Brynn made a strange sound in the back of her throat and took a gulp of wine. "I appreciate the gesture, but I don't need to be bought. When we make a compromise, it's important to me that both sides keep their word." She held her chin a bit higher. "And I'm not doing this for you. I'm doing this because I can't stand the thought of not being in Jacob's life." She squared her shoulders, making her point clear. He loved how despite their differences in size, she'd look him in the eye and argue toe to toe. Her ability to call him on his shit was only part of her appeal. Everything about her was clean and fresh. Her skin glowed and her cheeks carried a pinkish hue. The bar scene was no longer for him, stale and tiring like the women who always approached him. Layers of makeup, heavy perfume, and one common goal—to bed a SEAL. Brynn was refreshing and carried an air of innocence that fired up all his protective instincts.

"I'm sorry. I guess I wasn't thinking of it from that standpoint. But Brynn? I didn't buy those things for you. I bought them for me because I couldn't stand the thought of you leaving the place you call home without at least a memento of it." Her mouth gaped as he threw her words back. "So, aside from the library book, what loose ends do you need to tie up before we leave the state?" he asked, sitting with his body angled toward her.

Her expression grew pinched. "The van. I hadn't even thought of that. I'll need to drive it to Virginia." She tugged at her bottom lip. The action might have been involuntary, but it aroused him to no end. His body may have different ideas, but at least his mind had processed that Brynn was off-limits for too many reasons to count. If he lost her, he lost an excellent caretaker for Jacob. Plus, he didn't have the first clue how to tend to his brother's needs. Without Brynn, he and his brother would be left vulnerable. "I have another two months left on the apartment lease. I need to let the landlord know. He probably has an early termination fee, but I can always mail a check." She absently rolled her shoulders before taking a sip of her wine.

He didn't need her getting worked up about the move. She was already taking a huge chance, and her second-guessing herself was the last thing he wanted. "First, how attached are you to the van?"

"It's a means of transportation." She shrugged. "Point A to point B."

"I'm not saying this to be a prick…" He trailed off when she tilted her head. A strand of hair fell forward, trailing down the outer corner of her brow and playing against the apple of her left cheek.

"Usually if you have to lead with a statement like that, it means it's true." She raised one brow and leveled her gaze over the rim of her glass.

And hell if she didn't have a point there, but he didn't want her to think of him that way. So many others, his mother and women who had known the score before they jumped into his bed, had branded him as cold, suspicious, unlovable. She waited for a response, lips still poised along the rim of her glass.

"The van looks like it's a few drives from its final destination at the junkyard." He crossed his arms firmly over his chest, then cursed the action, which probably made him seem defensive.

Her cheeks puffed out and a spray of wine misted over his face. Her eyes went wide, her face tinged with pink, and she dissolved into laughter. "Oh. My. Gosh," she panted between breathless chuckles. "I'm so sorry."

"Didn't know I'd be traveling with a damn camel." He swiped his hands over his forehead and cheeks, flicking off the liquid. There was a smile plastered to his face. The tear that leaked from the corner of her eye did him in. The laughter started deep in his gut and tumbled out, shocking him. Not that he never chuckled at the occasional wisecrack Branch spouted off, but their line of work was serious. His world was often saturated with the worst humanity had to offer, and the lives he took, while necessary, scored his soul. Brynn's and Jacob's laughter was a floodlight shining through the dark. A beacon. Something hopeful.

When her laughter died, he sobered. She cleared her throat and looked away. "I really am sorry. That was an accident. The way you said it just sounded so…well, dramatic." Her slender, unpainted fingers plucked at a loose string on the robe. "I'm sorry."

"Don't apologize. I haven't laughed like that in a while, but in all seriousness, I'm buying a new accessible van when we get to Virginia." He didn't mention he'd be buying two.

It made more sense if both he and Brynn had the means to transport Jacob.

"That van was provided to me by your mother." She stood up and took her empty glass to the counter. "It's more yours and Jacob's than it is mine. Whatever you want to do with it is fine. I have no attachment to it."

Another way his mother had let Jacob down. Instead of buying him a safe means of transportation, she squandered all her inheritance. Brynn's mere presence tempered some of his anger, and she was returning to the couch. He was trying to be a gentleman, but he couldn't help but notice the sway of her hips when she walked, or how her shapely her long legs were. "All right, that's settled. And the apartment? The thought of you putting another dime in that landlord's pocket pisses me off. Let me take care of that for you. Please, Brynn."

She shook her head, and the strands framing her face swayed with the motion. Her bare feet were silent on the carpeted floor as she came to the couch. "I don't want any fights on my behalf," she said, sitting and pulling her legs beneath her once again.

He leaned forward. "Because he violated the terms established by the Department of Public Health for a rented dwelling, you're leaving the premises effective now. No fight will come of it, but mark my words, should the need arise, I will fight for you, Brynn."

Her brows scrunched together, as if she thought his statement was ridiculous. "You can try, but if it doesn't work out, I'm prepared to pay the rent because that's what I signed up to do."

He stared at her for a moment. She was so hellbent on doing the right thing, it drew him back to his questions about her past. "Is Jacob able to fly?" he asked, changing the subject. There was no way she was paying that landlord, but he'd keep that to himself.

"He has no flight restrictions, but we'll have to leave for the airport early in case he needs an additional security check, and I imagine it might take longer to board with a wheelchair. He's only flown once that I know of, before I worked with him. As far as when to leave, I have what I need for Jacob and me. I do have several calls I need to make to his medical supply company. They're the provider that sends enteral nutrition and things like new attachments for his feeding tube each month. I'll do some research in the morning and have them transfer his prescriptions to another company in the Virginia area."

"I'm happy to jump in where I can, even if it's just running last-minute errands or hanging out with Jacob while you get things squared away. My teammates are researching available housing close to the base. That's one of the things I wanted to discuss with you. My apartment isn't a good bet long-term, and I want to purchase permanent housing. You rented an apartment for two out of necessity, but you also mentioned living in the carriage house. What is your ideal situation? A condo or home of your own or staying in the same location as Jacob?"

Her cheeks flamed again, and his fingers itched to draw the pad of his thumb down the side of her face. "What are you thinking?"

"That I'm stupid not to consider that you may have a

girlfriend or wife who wouldn't want another woman constantly in her personal space. If that's the case, I can live off-site. Part of my arrangement with your mother was twenty-four-hour availability. She didn't have time to see to a child. Her addiction didn't allow for it. My room and board were part of the contract." She drew her legs up again, tucking them beneath her.

"What about days off?"

"At first, there was a block of time on Saturday when I would leave. I thought your mother wanted to spend time with her son. When I discovered she wasn't even visiting the carriage house, I started taking him with me everywhere. Taking care of Jacob is no hardship, Neo."

He scrubbed his hands over his face. "I'm not going to be a deadbeat brother. If I'm on US soil I intend to spend as much time with Jacob as I possibly can. If you want weekends off or need to do something during the week, so long as I'm stateside, it's not going to be a problem. I want to learn how to take care of my brother's medical needs, too, and I know my teammates will have my back on that. When I'm deployed, though, I won't be able to tell you where I'll be or how long I'll be gone. I might only have a few hours' notice before I'm on an airplane. Those are the times I'll need to make sure Jacob is covered around the clock. I'll leave it up to you whether you'd like to hire additional nurses. I have no doubt you'll vet them. And to answer your question, there's no way I'd be in your room this late if I had a woman."

The air between them charged with electricity. Oh yes, there was chemistry between them. She'd charmed him with her terrible singing voice and spontaneous dance moves the second he laid eyes on her. With each passing hour he liked her more and more. She was the worst person he could develop feelings for. Jacob needed her. Hell, he needed her, and he wasn't going to do anything to drive her away.

CHAPTER SIX

BRYNN HAD SLEPT like a rock. Something she hadn't thought possible after Neo left last night. He'd electrified her space when he passed the threshold and entered her room. A shiver of pleasure had feathered down her spine when he told her if he had a woman, he wouldn't be in her bedroom. Those words made her curious in ways she shouldn't be. Having his full attention on her alone was an intense experience, but having him in close proximity in the hotel room? Total sensory overload. With his invigorating scent in her nostrils, she'd suggested they regroup to discuss things in the morning. She couldn't help replaying the moment in her head. Thinking about him as anything other than her employer was wrong—he was Jacob's brother.

She woke this morning to a text from Neo. He'd left the hotel early to square away the apartment lease with her landlord, saying he'd meet them for breakfast in the hotel restaurant after he was finished. She'd meant what she said last night, though: she fully intended to pay the rent and she was fine with that. Another text had come in to let her know he was headed her way and was about ten minutes out. She liked how considerate he was. Instead of feeling smothered, it was nice to have someone care enough to send updates so she could plan accordingly. For what seemed like the hundredth time she chastised herself for letting her mind speculate about the kind of man he was rather than the kind of employer. Her relationship with Jacob and her livelihood depended on her ability to remain objective.

"Excited to see your brother this morning?" she asked as she backed Jacob's wheelchair onto the elevator. He turned his head toward her and smiled. Those big grins never failed to add an extra shot of sunlight to her day. She pressed the lobby button. Last night, at dinner, they'd talked to him about why they'd left the apartment and the plan to go with Neo back to his base, Fort Lorrie, in Virginia. They also told him about his mother's car accident. He was subdued for a while but then returned to his jovial disposition. His mother had spent so little time with him that she was virtually a stranger to the teen. The elevator pinged when they reached the lobby, and the doors slid open. She wheeled Jacob out and scanned the space. Chaise longues and oversized armchairs were spread beneath cascades of crystal from two chandeliers at the entrance. She'd never stayed in a hotel this luxurious. Her gaze landed on a man with straight dark hair sitting in an emerald crushed velvet chair with his nose buried in a newspaper. She stiffened. Her pulse kicked up a notch. No. Could it be him? She took one hesitant step back, then another. A tremor shook her hand as she reached for the buttons outside the elevator before her name echoed across the room.

"Brynn, Jacob!" Neo waved and began jogging in their direction. She looked back at the emerald chair, but the only thing sitting there was the discarded newspaper. A tendril of fear unfurled in her chest.

As Neo approached, his expression hardened. He greeted them both before his eyes narrowed. "Is everything okay? You looked startled."

"No, I'm fine. I thought I saw someone I knew, but it wasn't anyone. I'm probably just hungry." Now that Neo was with them, her stomach muscles relaxed, and she let out a quiet exhalation. She had just met Neo, but she couldn't deny he made her feel safe, which was strange because she didn't trust many people.

"Well, let's get you something to eat." They walked up to the restaurant, and the host brought them to a table, taking a seat away to make room for Jacob's wheelchair.

"What'll be this morning?" She grinned at Jacob, who was already eyeing her with rapt attention. He always chose scrambled eggs, but to be sure, she gave him options. "Pancakes?" Jacob stayed still, looking straight ahead. "Okay, not pancakes. Oatmeal?" He gave an exaggerated sigh.

"Geez, buddy. Tell us how you really feel." Neo's chuckle was a deep rumble that wrapped around her and sent flutters dancing through her stomach. A sound she would happily get lost in and one she was going to try to elicit at every opportunity.

"Omelet?" Now Jacob was chuckling, too. "French toast?" His body shook, and a tear streamed down his cheek. "All right, all right. Scrambled eggs and cheese?" Jacob turned his head to tell her yes, still wheezing with laughter, those bright eyes crinkling with humor.

"That laugh, man." Neo shook his head. "Nothing better." Their waitress brought over coffee, tea, and juice, and Brynn took a packet from her purse and began mixing it in

Jacob's apple juice.

"What's that?" Neo leaned forward and slid his chair closer to Jacob.

"We add this to all of Jacob's liquids to thicken them. Swallowing can be challenging and sometimes dangerous. If his drinks aren't the consistency of honey, he could aspirate, which can cause pneumonia."

Neo sat silently for a moment, studying her as she fixed the drink. "There's so much I don't know. I could hurt him unintentionally without even realizing it," he whispered.

"You'll learn. I can make a chart to put on the refrigerator." She could feel heat tingling along her cheeks. The way she said it made it seem intimate like they would be sharing the same spaces all the time. She really needed to get a grip. Her life had been wrought with enough insecurities—her safety, a place to belong, rejection. Those were the reasons she chose to be alone. Independence was the safest option. As long as she made smart choices and maintained a steady income, she'd never have to depend on anyone again.

"I'm happy you're coming home with me. You won't regret it." Now that sounded quite intimate, too, whether he realized it or not.

The waitress came back to the table and set down their plates. She had a sweet tooth and ordered the stuffed French toast, which was basically a dessert for breakfast. Cream cheese and strawberries were layered between sugar-dusted slices of bread piled high with whipped cream. She'd been surprised when Neo ordered the same thing before remembering he told her about the name Ransom and the chocolate chip cookies. She took turns taking bites of her French toast and helping Jacob eat his eggs.

"Can I try?" Neo placed down his fork and scooted his chair closer to Jacob.

"Of course." She passed him the spoon and busied herself with her own breakfast.

"Okay, Jacob. I'm going to give it a try. Won't be as good as Brynn here, but you'll let me know if I'm doing it wrong, yeah?"

Happiness fizzed to life within her, bubbling and bright, affirming her decision to make this drastic move to Virginia. This was Jacob's chance to get to know his brother. She wanted that for him. The connection was already there, their eyes shining with appreciation. Whether he knew it or not, Neo was already comfortable interacting with Jacob. He picked up his subtle communication skills as if he'd known him for months, not days. Many people looked at Jacob and only saw what was on the surface, but those who took the time to interact with him learned that just because he couldn't verbalize his thoughts didn't mean he couldn't communicate them. Because Jacob could only control his movements from the neck up, he used his eyes, smile, or a turn of his head to indicate what he wanted. Before she'd pulled him out of school, the special education department was researching other ways that Jacob might be able to communicate through the use of adaptive or assistive technology. That was something she was eager to see through in Virginia.

Neo spooned up some eggs, fumbling the utensil and dropping a bit onto the table. "Haven't made it to your mouth and already spilling." A peal of laughter ripped from

Jacob. "Hey, now. Cut me some slack here." It took Neo more than a few tries to get the hang of it, but he kept trying and didn't get discouraged or upset.

Warmth spread through her chest as Neo fell into a rhythm of feeding Jacob. He hunched close to his brother, rambling about this and that, trying his best to make Jacob laugh. Endearing. So beautiful to witness that the interaction burned inside her. At first glance, Neo was intimidating. A warrior with the jagged ridges and indentations of battle visible on his exposed skin. Monochromatic scenes and words were inked down both arms. More hidden beneath his shirt. She was curious about the ones concealed by denim and cotton. Heat struck her, taking her aback, and pooled like molten honey between her hips. Her body was having a ridiculous reaction to him. Still, she didn't know how to stop the light-headedness that had taken over. She wasn't experienced. Her only sexual interaction had been a fumbled attempt in a dorm room at college. The boy had been disappointed. She'd been relieved when he climbed off of her. Never had she been subjected to a pure visceral reaction to someone. Not until Neo.

"Excuse me." Her throat was as dry, and she stood and rushed to the bathroom. Her heart was hammering. Skin tight and uncomfortable. And an ache she hadn't the first clue how to get rid of pulsed at the juncture of her thighs. The mirror reflected all of that and more. Hot, flushed skin. Wide, aroused eyes. She gripped the sides of the sink and drew in a few breaths before splashing her face with cold water. The more time she puttered around in the bathroom, the more heat prickled her cheeks. Neo must think she was nuts. Maybe she was. She might be attracted to him, but she didn't need any complications. Especially with Jacob involved. She could always get another job, but Jacob was irreplaceable. On a sharp exhalation, she left the bathroom and headed back to their table.

"What's the plan for today?" she said the moment she pulled out her chair and sat.

"We can return the library book, then drive straight to the airport if you're both up for it." Neo's eyes were on her, carefully assessing. He knew there was a reason she'd left the table, but to his credit, he didn't ask. "There's a flight at three this afternoon."

The gravity of moving hundreds of miles south of Boston started to set in. Maybe it was crazy, but it was the first thing that had felt right in a long time. While she didn't trust others' intentions easily, something about Neo told her if she could ever trust someone it would be him. She couldn't keep wavering on her decision. It was either losing Jacob or starting fresh in a new area. No ties were holding her in Boston. "Okay."

"Yeah?" Neo continued to stare at her, even after she'd nodded. When he seemed to find what he was looking for in her expression, he nodded and turned to his brother. "And what about you?" Jacob made a high-pitched squeal, and they both laughed. "He's all in."

Brynn picked up her now-cooled tea. "I never asked you about the rental agreement."

Neo sat back in his chair. "Didn't give me a hassle. The fact that the fire department was there helped, too. As soon as I started talking about violations of the rental agreement, the fire chief homed in on our conversation, and the landlord agreed to everything just to shut me up. No early termination fees. You're free."

"Fire department?" The fine hairs on the back of her neck rose. "Did something happen?"

"Sounded like someone threw a lit cigarette in the trash piled up in the hall in the early morning hours. The fire department contained it. No one was hurt."

"Oh my God." She'd done the best she could for Jacob with her limited financial resources, but if Neo hadn't come when he did, if the fire department couldn't put out the blaze, Jacob could've been hurt or worse.

"Brynn, look at me."

She met his gaze even though the French toast had soured in her stomach.

"Whatever is going on in your head right now, shut it down. Jacob's safe and cared for because of you. Don't forget that. You'll never have to see that apartment building again, and you'll sure as hell never be in a financial bind like that again. I will not turn my back on either of you."

His words warmed her, settling her choppy stomach. He reached across the table and engulfed her hand in his own. Her body immediately settled, making room for a spark to tingle along her skin where his rough palm cocooned her hand. The angle gave her a clear view of his forearm and the tattoo there. A soldier walking into battle. A scene of chaos in smoky gray tones. The man's head was bent, but his shoulders were squared like he was aware of his own mortality once he stepped forth into hell. The scene spoke of death and sacrifice. A wall of emotion wedged in her throat.

Flowers speared from the ground near the soldier's feet. Bold crimson-orange blossoms with paper-thin petals. Poppies.

She involuntarily lifted her other hand and traced her fingertips over the flowers. Neo stiffened, then relaxed. Goose bumps popped up along his skin everywhere she touched, but she couldn't seem to make herself stop. "I always thought my nana hated poppies because she'd weep whenever she came across them, but she insisted she loved them. That they were important for her to see because they helped her remember what hatred could do to people and families. Her father served in the British forces during World War One. He survived the horrors of war only to be murdered a month after returning home to a nationalist Ireland. Thousands of veterans returned to a country that shunned them and was hostile and cruel."

"I'm sorry." He brushed his thumb back and forth over her skin. "The pain one person can inflict on another is devastating. Especially in times of war."

"Nana took after her father. She was a warrior in her own way. Always stood up for what and who she believed in." The only person in her life who had ever made a stand for her was her grandmother. Nana had given up her homeland, family, and retirement to ensure Brynn was safe from her brother. Her older sibling had a wicked streak. One her parents refused to acknowledge or believe. Nana believed her, though, and she put as much distance between her and Fergus as possible. She didn't believe much in fate or divine intervention, but those poppies on Neo's forearm made her feel close to her grandmother, as though she was telling Brynn it was safe to trust this man. That he was part of her path.

"Who was he?"

"What makes you think he's gone?"

"His posture. I just thought…the way he's positioned makes me think he knew his fate before ever charging into the fight, yet he did it anyway."

"Yes." Neo glanced at Jacob, who had dozed off after breakfast. His morning medications had kicked in, so he would nap for an hour at least. "That's Scooter. He was young and passionate about serving his country. We were on a mission that went sideways, and he sacrificed himself so the rest of the team could complete our objective."

"Neo," she whispered, squeezing his hand with her own. "I'm so sorry."

He looked down at their intertwined hands before his startling eyes met hers. "His sacrifice marked me in ways I can't begin to describe. Everything I feel about what he did is a contradiction. Anger that he made that decision when the team could've aborted or found another way. Grateful because of what we were able to accomplish because he decided to take that choice out of our hands. Lives were saved because of him, but the cost was so damned high. I guess it's like life in a way. The yin and yang. Good and bad. Happiness and despair. One thing never exists without the other."

CHAPTER SEVEN

NEO NEVER TALKED about Scooter's sacrifice outside the Teams. The experience had gutted him; bringing it up was like packing salt into an infected wound. Yet he wanted to confide in Brynn. He found his own pain reflected in her eyes as she shared that burden with him, her strong hand gripping his, that melodic voice soothing the fractured spaces in his heart. He loved how her voice sounded. He'd replay the cadence in his head on missions to lull him into sleep. Right or wrong, in a matter of a few days, Brynn had gotten under his skin. He'd been unable to take his eyes off her as she and Jacob played a game on his iPad after takeoff, heads bent close together, giggling every so often.

"Are you all right?" Brynn tentatively touched his arm. Little did she know the simple gesture made his pulse pound.

He nodded. "Is it normal for Jacob to sleep so much?" His brother was now snoring next to Brynn. A drink cart rumbled down the narrow center aisle, overstacked plastic cups teetering with the motion.

"Yes. His antiseizure medication makes him drowsy. He takes a few short naps each day." Brynn swept her hair over her shoulder. The dark strands were glossy and straight, made to bury his hands into. Self-control had been drilled into him by the Navy, so the intense urge to reach out and touch startled him.

He gripped his hands together in his lap to keep them from reaching out of their own accord. "Does he still have them? The seizures?"

"Sometimes. If he's developing an illness or is overstimulated by certain lights, it's still possible, even with the medication." She looked to her right to check on Jacob, then focused her attention back on him.

"And if that happens?" Calm was in his nature, but thoughts of his little brother having a seizure? His shoulders and stomach were tight just having this conversation. For the millionth time, he was thankful Brynn was at his side.

"We give him space, make sure there is nothing he can roll into, and start timing. Anything that nears five minutes, we call emergency services. I also carry medication in the front pouch of his backpack anywhere we go. We'd use it after calling for an ambulance."

He couldn't stop himself from grabbing her hand. Soft, strong, and so fucking sweet. "Have I thanked you for coming with us?"

"Maybe a few times." When she smiled, those plump lips tipped up, her eyes lit with warmth, and the apples of her cheeks flushed. Goddamn.

"If something bothers you or you're unhappy with any part of our agreement, will you promise to talk to me?"

"Okay." She nodded. Their conversation was stalled as the flight attendant asked if they'd like a drink or snack. They passed Brynn a Sprite, him a water, and orange juice for when Jacob woke up.

"I know it's not great for me, but Sprite's my guilty

pleasure." She took a sip and closed her eyes.

"Just Sprite? Anything else I should know about?" He wanted to know her every guilty pleasure and provide them in abundance.

Her cheeks flamed, and his cock twitched in his jeans. He hadn't meant the question to come across as sexual, but the color creeping up her neck and the way her pupils dilated, pools of black spilling over into blue, told him that's where her mind had gone. Fuck. Years had passed without him being interested in a woman, and now one he'd just met—his brother's nurse—was taking his common sense and systematically disintegrating every honorable intention he possessed. There was nothing wrong with getting to know the woman who would be helping Jacob. He just needed to remember there was a hard line, and crossing it would have consequences he wasn't prepared to deal with.

She cleared her throat, grabbing his attention. "Hooded sweatshirts, ugly dogs, and peculiar teapots. What about you?" She lifted her can of soda and poured half of it over the cup of ice provided.

A deep chuckle erupted from his throat. "Adrenaline highs, and macaroni and cheese. Strong black coffee, my KA-BAR knife, and a pretty voice with a hint of an Irish brogue." There was that blush again. His body temperature ratcheted up a few degrees. As his lust was growing, so was his stupidity. She wasn't a woman he could innocently flirt with. Those shy and sweet visceral reactions she responded with were way too appealing. The emotions that played out on her face weren't guarded or practiced. In his line of work, he didn't see much innocence or softness. Everyone could lock their shit down at a moment's notice and do what needed to be done to accomplish a mission. Brynn didn't conceal a thing. It was refreshing. Dangerous.

"Gonna stretch my legs." He unbuckled and moved around Brynn and a still-sleeping Jacob. Getting lost in intense physical activity might temper his attraction, but on an airplane of this size, he'd have to make do with a walk to the bathroom. Without being near Brynn's light lavender scent, the canned air of the cabin was stale. A woman's overpowering floral perfume choked him. Beneath it was hints of sour milk and sweat—none of it appealing. He used the vacant bathroom, barely able to turn around in the cramped stall, to splash his face with cold water. He did some breathing exercises to rein in his emotions and then prepared to go back to his seat. When he emerged from the lavatory, there was a commotion in the center of the airplane. An older man was in the aisle on his knees. His face had a purplish hue, and he gestured wildly at his throat. A woman was screaming.

A flash of dark hair swayed behind the man. Brynn was so small compared to the distressed traveler, he hadn't spotted her at first, but she was there, wrapping her arms around the man's thick waist, thrusting up with her balled fists. A crowd had gathered as he pushed down the carpeted aisle. Brynn was relentless, using the Heimlich maneuver over and over. Someone at the front of the mob gasped, then shrieked as something flew from the man's mouth and into the noisy passengers. The man collapsed, knocking into Brynn and sending her backward.

"Move," he barked and the crowd parted. The hysterical

woman was kneeling beside the man, patting his back. He passed them and crouched near Brynn, helping her to her feet. "You all right, Wonder Woman?"

"Aside from a sore butt, yes, fine." He started to guide her back to their seats. The wild-eyed woman beside the man Brynn had saved jumped to her feet. Her skin was ruddy and pockmarked, and he could smell the alcohol on her breath.

"My husband was in a recent car accident. You wrenched his back."

He immediately pushed Brynn behind him. "Ma'am, your husband was choking. The woman you're raising your voice to is a registered nurse who saved his life."

"She reaggravated his injuries. Used too much force." The woman's eyes were glassy as she advanced on them.

He held out a hand to stop her forward progress. "Ma'am. You need to take a step back."

Several flight attendants had gathered around. One was helping the man stand to his feet, and the other two flanked the irate wife.

The man turned to face them. "Thank you for your help."

"Thank her? She nearly broke you in two." The statement was laughable, given Brynn's stature compared to the man she'd helped.

"But I—" The man's jowls wobbled.

"Charles, shut your mouth. Back to the seat." Her husband bowed his head, cowed by his wife, and shuffled away with the flight attendant. "The moment we get off this airplane, I'll consult our lawyer."

He'd had enough of the woman's ungrateful noise, but

she tucked her claws away and returned to her seat a few rows behind them.

"I'm pissed as hell that lady would complain after you saved her husband's life, but you don't seem fazed. Why is that?" He had wanted to rail at the woman and let her know she was despicable for accusing Brynn of hurting her husband when she'd saved his life. His hands were trembling, fury coursing through him.

"Hey." Brynn looked down at his balled fists and touched his arm. "That wasn't an abnormal reaction. I was an emergency room nurse before I started working with your brother. Emotions are high when someone you love is hurting, and while we might not understand why someone would yell and carry on at the wrong people, sometimes that's what happens. She was also intoxicated. The important thing is the man's airway is cleared. I'm not concerned about anything else at the moment, so you shouldn't be either."

He scrubbed his hands down his face. Maybe Brynn should've been a SEAL. She was totally at peace with what had just gone down. He was far from it. The rest of the trip continued without incident, and when they landed, Jacob was wide awake. Brynn had discreetly fed him, pouring liquid through a syringe into a small tube connected to a port in his belly. Once they stepped out of the gate terminal, his team was waiting. Whether they were on a mission or not, they had each other's backs. From helping to locate his brother to connecting him with a real estate agent and sending him text messages of dozens of listings, to meeting them at the airport, they showed their support.

"This must be the Jacob we've been hearing all about."

Branch crouched by his brother's wheelchair as passengers rushed past with their luggage. He was by far the best with children out of their group. He had a soft spot for kids and was always looking out for the locals when they were on a mission. He'd bought food from a marketplace and distributed it to kids wandering the dusty streets more than once. Jacob locked eyes with him and smiled. "Nice to meet you, man. Welcome to the family." Branch stood, clapped him on the back, and turned his attention to Brynn. "Thanks for accompanying these boys home." He offered his hand to Brynn, and she took it. "Branch. Nice to meet you."

"I'm Brynn. Jacob's nurse."

He didn't miss how Brynn stepped closer to him. Her trust made him feel ten feet tall.

"I'd be happy to show you around the area sometime." Branch smiled, dimples indenting both cheeks.

He was scowling at the exchange. He had no claim to Brynn, but something white-hot and ugly was bubbling in his gut. Jealousy was new for him, and he didn't like it one bit, but damn if he didn't want to give Branch a shove and tell him to keep his dirty hands to himself. When Branch didn't immediately let go of her hand, he put his arm around Brynn's shoulder like a fucking Neanderthal. What was with him?

Branch's eyes twinkled with humor while Brynn's clouded with confusion.

You and me both.

She gazed up at him. "Everything okay?"

Silver smirked but wisely kept his mouth shut. Joker wore a scowl on his face, probably working every angle on how Brynn was out to get him.

"Yeah." He sucked in a breath, grounding himself. "All good. That old SOB over there is Silver. He's the one who helped me locate Jacob. That guy with the pissy look on his face is Joker." His team had seen his gesture of wrapping his arm around Brynn for what it was—he might have no claim to her at this moment, but he was sure as hell interested. Just because she was off-limits to him didn't mean he wanted his friends vying for her attention. Silver introduced himself to Jacob, taking Branch's lead and crouching down so they were at eye level.

"How long are you staying?" Joker took a few steps toward them and crossed his arms over his chest. His question was harmless enough, but he understood what Joker was really doing. Being an ass. Pushing the envelope.

Brynn glanced up at him, then back at Joker. "I go where Jacob goes. If he's staying, you'll be seeing a lot of me."

Neo grinned at the stubborn tilt of her chin. Just like their first meeting when he barged into her apartment, her features steeled with determination, and fire danced in her eyes.

"Help me get the bags from luggage claim, yeah?" Joker stared at him for a moment, then nodded.

"Welcome home." Joker nodded at Jacob, but passed right by Brynn as he followed Neo.

"We won't miss you," Branch called when they were a few feet away. "We'll all relax and get to know each other." He flashed those goddamn dimples at Brynn again.

"You and I are gonna have words," he muttered under his breath and shook his head. When they were out of earshot, he whirled on Joker. So far, Silver was the only one who hadn't annoyed the hell out of him in the last ten minutes. "What the fuck was that?"

"I'm looking out for you, brother. You don't know this woman. I get that she was taking care of Jacob, that she's a nurse. But goddamn, people aren't always what they seem. What if she robs you blind and takes off when we're on a mission? Leaves Jacob?"

"When she thought Jacob was in danger when I showed up unannounced, she shielded him. She was ready to stand in front of him and fight rather than let me get to him. Later, when she discovered I planned to bring him home, she was fucking gutted. Let's not forget that she went months without pay, living off her savings to care for him. That tells me all I need to know about the kind of person she is."

"She's not just a person to you. I saw how you acted. You want to fu—"

"Careful," he all but growled. When it came to women, Joker always thought the worst. He could only cut him so much slack for his screwed-up childhood. Disrespecting Brynn was crossing a hard line. "She's gotten under my skin, yes, but I'm not going to jeopardize her relationship with Jacob. The kid loves her like a mother. Actually, she's the only one he's ever had. I will not tolerate you being an ass. She's part of the team now, whether you like it or not."

Silence hung in the air between them until Joker wordlessly turned and stalked toward the baggage claim. He raked his fingers through his cropped hair and prayed he'd be able to hold fast to his word.

CHAPTER EIGHT

THERE WAS NO way she was going to be able to stay true to her promise of keeping Neo at arm's length. Not if he continued to cast her heated stares and wrap his arm around her shoulders. The gesture had been a surprise, but not one that was unwelcome. Even after a day of travel, she could still detect the hint of soap on his skin. She had to consciously stop herself from breathing him in—or the urge to tuck into his side.

It wasn't just his scent that made her want to be close to him. Perhaps it was his imposing size or his job description. Still, when she was walking close to Neo, it was like having an invisible shield separating them from the rest of the population. People gave Neo a wide berth. It had been a long time since she'd been through the rigors of air travel and her limbs were heavy with exhaustion. Add in meeting three strangers to that, and it was all a bit overwhelming.

Right now, she could hardly hear the men above the onslaught of sounds. Some loud and jarring. Coughs and loud conversations. Babies crying and the honk of a cart whizzing through the crowd. Others were more muted, contributing to the larger cacophony buzzing in her ears. Ruffling papers and the click of heels. Luggage wheels spinning along the tile and self-serve kiosks spitting out printed tickets.

So far, Branch and Silver had been welcoming to both her and Jacob. The man called Joker? Not so much. At least not to her. He was kind to Jacob, and really, that was what mattered most. Things would've been different if he hadn't been, but there were shadows in the man's eyes that she thought might contribute to his unease. Perhaps he just needed time to adjust.

"Don't worry about Joker." Silver looked up from where he was crouched next to Jacob. He had close-cut blond hair and a few days' worth of stubble, a nose that had been broken a time or two, and sincerity in his eyes. "He's forgetting that Neo is good at reading people. That he never would've brought you here if it weren't for your connection to his brother. Give him time, but don't let him be an ass."

"I'm sure Neo's putting him in his place as we speak." Branch was sitting with his elbows resting on his knees. He might look harmless and carefree, but like the other men, he had a warrior's build. One that she was sure could change from easygoing to battle-ready with the flip of a switch. She didn't fear them, though—even Joker. People with nefarious intentions didn't have to be big and imposing. Their minds were the worst weapon.

"I don't want to cause some kind of rift. I can take care of myself." She crossed her arms around her waist. Fracturing relationships was one of her specialties.

"He'll get over it. Give him a few days. He's got some shit to deal with that has nothing to do with you or Jacob, but that doesn't make it right." He glanced into the congested crowd toward the baggage claim. Like Neo, he seemed to constantly scan his surroundings, quietly assessing.

"Don't we all," she murmured. Her own parents had been willing to toss her to the side when she opened up about her brother's abuse. Their reaction was the total opposite of what she expected. Instead of helping her, they accused her of lying. Of being jealous of his achievements. She was intimately aware that blood was no thicker than water.

"So you and Neo, huh?" Branch shot her an affable grin as he redirected the conversation.

"Branch isn't exactly known for his subtlety." Silver rolled his eyes.

There was no denying that something had sparked in her heart when Neo was near. A recognition of sorts. A pull from deep within. She shook her head and raised a brow. "No. Neo's hired me to watch over his brother's medical needs and ensure the relocation is smooth." She shifted in the hard seat of the lounge area.

"Speaking of relocation, me and the guys have some properties for you to check out tomorrow. Some might need modifications, but we tried to stick close to what Neo asked for. There's one in particular that I'm excited for you guys to see." He flashed her a grin, stood up, and started walking away from the lounge area.

"Where did he go?" By the way Jacob searched the crowd, she could tell he was wondering the same thing.

"Ah. Well, where Joker sucks with people, Branch more than makes up for it. He's also the most distractible and impulsive of the group. Probably saw something shiny or someone who needed a hand." Silver lifted his chin toward the security checkpoint. Branch was hauling a rolling carry-on in one hand and a pet cage in another. Hearing the conversation from this distance was impossible, but Branch's easy smile as he chatted to the elderly man he was assisting wasn't forced. The man genuinely liked helping others.

"So Joker is the antisocial one," she said. "Branch is the squirrel—"

"Squirrel?" A deep chuckle rumbled through Silver.

"Yeah. A squirrel sees a nut; no matter what it's doing, it's off on the hunt. Jumps down from its branch, and it's gone."

He gave Jacob a broad smile and was given one in return. "All right. I'm following what your nurse is saying now."

"Right, so what does that make Neo? And you? Why Silver?" She suddenly had so many questions about the group's dynamic. Jacob cackled at her string of inquiries, and his arms and legs shook involuntarily.

"Hey, you okay?" Silver looked frantically from her to Jacob.

"He's fine. Right, Jacob?" She laid her hands gently just above his knees to ease the trembling. "Sometimes, when he gets excited or overstimulated, his body shakes. It's typical of his condition."

"You'll have to tell us if there are any medical warning signs to look for. That way, we can all keep an eye out."

She nodded. "I'm happy Jacob will have good people in his life. He deserves that."

"We're a family. Brothers. If Neo trusts you enough to care for his brother, you're in that circle, too." Silver fastened his gaze on her. "We watch each other's backs, and that includes at home as well as overseas. Now to answer your questions. Neo is cold and calculating. If a hard decision needs to be made, he's the most apt to wield the sword. I'm the old man. Boys thought it would be funny to nickname me Silver because I'm fifteen years their senior."

She scrunched her nose. "You don't have much gray in your hair for a silver fox."

"Don't have much hair at all, darlin'." A small smile tilted his lips.

"And I've seen a lot of emotions from Neo in the past two days, but cold and calculating haven't made the list once." She hated that Neo saw himself that way. Shae had always referred to her oldest son as a cold bastard who didn't care if she lived or died. Who never visited his mother. Now she understood why she never said she was disappointed he didn't visit his mom or brother. Shae had never contacted Neo to tell him that Jacob existed.

"That's how I know you're different." Silver's voice held a quiet intensity.

"What do you mean?" Her stomach fluttered.

"You said you've seen a lot of emotion." He shook his head. "That's not Neo. At least the man he shows to others. We see his other sides—the dry sense of humor, the profound hit he takes each time he's forced to make a difficult choice, the loyalty—but we see that only because he lets us. Because we've bled and suffered together." Silver drew in a quick breath. "Maybe it's meeting Jacob. Maybe it's a connection he feels with you or a combination of both, but he's letting you see him. He's giving you a glimpse of the one thing he doesn't dare show in battle. The one thing he isn't prepared to lose."

Brynn hesitated, then asked, "What's that?"

"His soul." He stood from his crouched position by Jacob's chair. The crowd had thinned, and Neo approached them with a duffel swung over his left shoulder. Behind him, Joker dragged the rolling bag.

"Everything okay?" Neo asked as he got closer. His stare was focused on her alone. He was a lot of things—intense. Stubborn. A born protector. But cold and ruthless? Not the man she'd been getting to know. Maybe she'd briefly thought him those things, but now, she couldn't imagine how she had.

"Everything's good." She tried to look for the callous and the hard, but his eyes seemed to soften when they landed on her and Jacob. "Thanks for getting the bags."

"Branch is helping a man through security. Joker and I will walk you out to the car, and he can meet up with us in the parking lot." Silver gripped the handles of Jacob's wheelchair. "Mind if I…?" he asked her.

"You'll have to ask Jacob." She was thrilled Neo's team was being hands-on with Jacob, but they didn't need to address her if they had a question for him. He made his own choices and had strong opinions to share, so long as you knew how to identify his tells.

"Sorry, man." Silver circled to the front of Jacob. "Won't happen again. Unless you want to do something illegal—then I might need to ask Nurse Brynn first. Okay if I wheel you?"

Jacob turned his head and chuckled, likely at the notion of doing something he shouldn't with Silver as a backup. "That was his way of saying yes."

"Awesome. You like to go fast?"

Jacob tilted his head back and let out a squeal that could only be described as pure delight.

Neo mussed his brother's hair, a genuine smile crashing over his face. "I think that was a hell yeah."

"Let's do it, then." Silver took off, weaving through the crowd right out the automatic sliding glass doors. Her breath hitched until the sound of Jacob's laughter riding over the other noise in the airport hit her square in the chest. Parts of this move might take work. Might be out of her comfort zone, but what they were getting in return far exceeded the growing pains. Jacob was getting a family. Four brothers who would have his best interests at heart. Joker followed them at a slower pace, pulling one of the bags behind him.

"Don't worry." Neo placed his hand on the middle of her back, and the urge to lean into the comfort of his touch caught her off guard. "He's in good hands. We'll meet them out there."

She glanced up at him. "At least let me take the bag, then."

"Not a chance." The way he whispered the words almost intimately made a shiver of pleasure skate down her spine.

Neo started to walk, but she reached out and grabbed his forearm. The one painted with poppies and the tribute to his friend. She half expected him to pull away, but he didn't. "I wasn't sure if I made the right decision to come here. Not really." Heat began prickling her cheeks, but she continued to meet his unwavering gaze. "Until now."

"It took a big leap of faith to come here with a man you'd just met. I won't betray the trust you've so freely given. Won't give you a reason to regret that decision. And I'm happy as hell you decided to come with us." He bent down and pressed his lips to the top of her head. His chest rose as he inhaled like he was cataloging the scent of her hair. Their close proximity had all her nerve endings firing at once, making her dizzy and breathless. Making her want more than she should.

CHAPTER NINE

NEO OPENED HIS eyes and listened for what had woken him. His bedroom was still encased in darkness, and the neon blue numbers on the digital clock read two o'clock in the morning. They were at his apartment in Virginia. His friends, all but Joker, had overstayed their welcome, hanging out with Jacob on the couch, shooting the shit while he helped Brynn unpack and hook up his brother's medical equipment. At midnight, Jacob was still thoroughly wired, but he could see the exhaustion weighing on Brynn and had kicked his buddies out.

The mattress was quiet beneath him as he sat up and slipped out from beneath his blanket. A low moan echoed through the dark. His breath stalled before his heart started racing. Calm and deadly was his usual MO, but now there were two people he cared about under his roof. He flung open his door and burst into the hallway. It took him only a moment to realize the sound was crying. Jacob's room was first, but that's not where the noise came from, so he bypassed it and walked straight to Brynn's room. He opened the door without knocking, too concerned for privacy, and flipped the bedside lamp on.

"Brynn, what's wrong?"

She sobbed again and circled into a tight ball, squeezing

the stuffed seahorse he'd given her like a vise. The sheets were a tangled mess on the floor, and despite the air conditioning, a sheen of sweat coated her pale skin.

He rounded the bed and crouched down. "Hey, it's Neo. You're having a bad dream. Brynn?" He shook her lightly when she didn't respond. Tears were trickling down her cheeks, and he was close enough now to see she was trembling. He swore and grabbed the sheet and blanket off the floor, tucking it around her.

"No. Stop hurting me."

Neo froze, his insides crackling into ice. This wasn't a bad dream, but a nightmare. And by her visceral reaction, she was reliving something she'd been through. He never took pleasure in killing, but her cries made him want to destroy whoever had hurt her. The pleas torn from her lips were excruciating, each like a sickening, physical blow.

"Brynn." He tried rousing her again, but she just recoiled. Going against everything he had learned, he climbed into the bed behind her and pulled her against him. "It's Neo. I've got you," he whispered in her ear. "You're in my apartment. Jacob's in the room next to you. I won't let anything touch you."

She stilled before turning over and scrambling into his arms, her face pressed against his bare chest. He automatically wrapped around her, a leg over her outer thigh and his arms around her back and tucked beneath her waist.

"It's you." She hiccupped and went boneless against him. "You, not him. Safe when you have me," she murmured, voice thick with sleep. On some internal level, Brynn trusted him to keep her safe. Tension built and expanded in his chest until it fractured and burst, filling him with blinding warmth and a satisfaction that he'd only experienced at the end of a successful mission.

Serving his country was no longer his only objective. Keeping Brynn and his little brother safe was a new kind of mission. Protecting them from a faceless enemy wasn't ideal, though. Brynn would have to open up to him about her past trauma and share if the presence of a threat was still possible. For the next three hours, Brynn slept, snuggling so close she was nearly wedged beneath him. Her soft breaths played against his skin while the lavender scent of her hair enveloped him. He'd never slept with a woman overnight before. Not once in his thirty-two years on this Earth had he experienced the contentment that came with holding someone special close. No-strings-attached sex was all he ever allowed himself. He'd never had an example of a healthy relationship growing up. He didn't want to drag someone into his dysfunction or, just as bad, let someone get close who was just like his mother. Now that he'd had Brynn tucked against him, he wasn't sure he could go back to sleeping alone.

At five o'clock, he snuck out of her bedroom and stripped off his sleep pants, trading them for shorts. He needed to clear his head with the sweat of a long run. As he passed Jacob's room, the sound of laughter stopped him. He knocked, then opened the door. His brother was wide awake in his bed, glancing around at the new surroundings. On a whim, Neo crossed the room to Jacob.

"What's going on in here?" he teased. "Brynn did say you were a night owl, but you seemed to be sleeping pretty well last night." He was rewarded with a brilliant smile. One that turned Jacob's eyes more of a golden green.

He chuckled, his whole body heaving with the motion. Jacob's body might be small, but his joy was infectious, and his spirit was larger than life. For the first time, he was thankful for his mother. Despite her hatred of him, one that ran so deep she refused to tell him about his brother, she was the reason he had Jacob in his life. "Wanna run with me?" He wanted time with his brother, and he'd witnessed how Jacob had been in his glory, racing through the parking lot with Silver. He moved his head so fast that Neo burst out laughing. "Okay, then." It took him longer to change and dress Jacob than it did Brynn, but he figured he'd get the hang of things with time. He buckled Jacob into his chair and left a note for Brynn on the kitchen table. The guys would meet them at noon at the first house they were touring. They could run downtown, grab some bagels and coffee, and jog back within an hour. Brynn might even be asleep when they returned. It had been a late night for both of them, but he was used to catching sleep at odd hours and going without for days.

They took the elevator down to the first floor and stepped outside the building. The early morning air was still cool, and dew beaded over the grass, making it sparkle beneath the bright light. His shoes slapped against the pavement, and he gripped the handlebars of the wheelchair. The air got warmer as they continued to run. After a mile, Neo slowed to a brisk walk to check on Jacob. He hadn't heard a peep out of him since the run began. He stepped out in front of the chair, and his heart swelled when Jacob's jubilant grin came into view. He was just enjoying the ride.

Exactly an hour later, they arrived back at the apartment. He was drenched in sweat and much clearer-headed than he'd been that morning when Brynn's warm body had been cuddled into him. When they entered the apartment, the shower was running. The image of Brynn's body slicked with water, her dark hair dripping down her bare back, rushed into his head before he could stop it. Heat spiked low in his gut, and his cock flexed against the thin material of his running shorts. The last thing he needed was for Brynn to leave the shower to find him standing half-mast in the small hallway. Especially if she remembered how he held her throughout the night.

So much for wishful thinking. The handle on the bathroom door opened, and Brynn stepped out, wrapped in a conservative white robe. He was intimately aware of the body beneath the terry cloth material—soft, luscious, and a perfect fit against him.

"Hey, sleepyhead." His voice was far too gritty to mistake the desire coating his words.

"Good morning." She glanced down at the floor. "You two have good timing. I'll make your scrambled eggs, Jacob, then we can do your breathing treatments before you start your house hunting." She wrapped her arms around her waist.

"You mean we. Take your time getting dressed. I'll get the eggs going. We brought home some bagels, Sprite, and coffee, so you can help yourself. Would you like some eggs?" He didn't like the way she was hiding from him. Her hair was curtained around her face, and she made no moves to push it back out of her eyes. Maybe she remembered bits and pieces from the night before. He wanted to tell her with certainty she had nothing to be ashamed of.

Her throat bobbed, and her arms fell to her sides. "I'm okay. Thanks." Then she turned and scurried down the hall. Whether the nightmare had shaken her, him being in her bed, or a combination of both, Brynn was on edge. She'd trusted him last night, but would she confide him now?

He was just finishing feeding Jacob his breakfast when Brynn walked into the kitchen, looking less vulnerable than she had in the hallway earlier. Good. Although he didn't want her to hide from him, he was glad some of her armor was back in place. He understood all too well how it felt to be stripped bare. The week of briefings after they returned from the mission where Scooter had sacrificed himself was the worst time of his life. Every action the team made was studied under a microscope. They'd left the country with six SEALs. Six beating hearts. They returned six SEALs, but only five hearts still beat. The guilt of losing a man had choked him until he'd wanted to claw at his own throat just to get some fucking air.

Once Brynn set Jacob up with his breathing treatments and a movie, she returned to the kitchen and began toasting one of the bagels. He was pleased she was eating after the night before. "Neo." She rubbed a hand over her chest. "Did…did I wake you last night?"

"Yes. I heard you crying. I tried to wake you, but nothing was working. I climbed into bed with you and held you."

She tugged at her bottom lip with her teeth. "I'm sorry."

He stood from the chair at the kitchen table, nearly

knocking it back, and went to her. "You don't have a damn thing to be sorry for." His fingers itched to cup her face as he told her everything would be okay. He didn't make promises he couldn't keep, though, and he had no idea what he was up against. All he knew was if someone was after her, they'd have to put him down to get to Brynn.

"It's just that it was my first night in a new place, and it was a long day." The bagel popped up from the toaster, but Brynn didn't seem to notice.

"How often do they happen?"

"Mostly when there are a lot of changes in my life or something pops up that makes me remember…"

"Remember what?" he said, keeping his tone gentle.

She opened her mouth to speak, then closed it again. A loud knock sounded on the door, and she flinched. His team was always so goddamn punctual.

"Brynn, whatever it is, I want to help you. Even if it's just having a sounding board. Someone to shoulder some of the weight. We haven't known each other long, but I think it's undeniable we have a connection. You're part of the team. Part of the family now. I hope you can trust me to take some of the burden that haunts your dreams." The knock came again, louder this time.

"Hold it," he barked, crossing the room to fling open the door.

"Whoa. Wrong side of the bed today?" Joker stepped inside, and Neo punched him in the shoulder. The impact wasn't hard, but it wasn't necessarily friendly either. He'd been annoyed at how he responded to Brynn yesterday.

"You're ten minutes early."

"Go back to whatever you were doing. Won't even notice I'm here." Joker made his way to the living room, where he joined Jacob.

Brynn was now sitting at the table, her bagel untouched. He pulled out a chair and angled it toward her. "Listen," he said, sitting down. "Whatever it is, I have your back. When we get home later, will you talk to me?"

"I'll think about it." Her voice was quiet. Unsure. The tone didn't give him much confidence that she'd confide in him.

"If there's something going on, an abusive ex or something you've gotten into and can't get out of, I need to know about it. I have to think about Jacob's safety, too, and between me and my teammates, we're a formidable defense. I can't help you, though, if you won't tell me. That also means I can't protect my brother the way he deserves to be protected."

She flinched back, cheeks reddening. "Don't you think I've thought of Jacob's safety? That if I were in trouble or in danger I would've brought it to Jacob's doorstep? You said trust wasn't something that came easily to either or us. I understand that. If you need to look into my records, fine."

"I have a feeling I won't find what I'm after in your records. I want the story that's not there. The reason you were having a flashback last night. The reason you let me hold you through the night."

"And that story is mine to tell if and when I'm ready, but I can assure you there's no danger to Jacob. I've done nothing wrong—haven't broken any laws or made questionable decisions I should be ashamed of."

"My living is assessing danger and taking calculated risks, but I need to know for my own peace of mind that Jacob's not in danger. Please, Brynn."

The flash of hurt in her eyes was the last thing he saw before she turned her back on him and left the room. He didn't know what had happened to Brynn, but one thing was certain, she wasn't going to be letting him comfort her again anytime soon. She was mad and hurt, and while he could understand her thought process, protecting was in his blood. He wanted to ensure Brynn and Jacob were both safe. He'd bide his time, but he hoped like hell last night wasn't the first and last time he'd hold her close.

CHAPTER TEN

B RYNN STOOD IN the driveway of a rambling ranch-style home and gawked. They'd been touring homes all day but nothing had been an ideal location for Jacob. The homes had been beautiful, but each would've required expensive updates to make them accessible.

"This is the one I'm most excited for you guys to see." Branch stood beside her, surveying the property. Silver, Joker, Neo, and Jacob were already making their way up the path leading to the house. "I had hoped the real estate agent could make it the first showing, but it didn't work out."

"It's beautiful." The combination of stone, wood, and glass was striking, as was the lush green lawn and meticulously arranged garden beds. What caught her eye the most, though, was the ramp that curved to the front door.

"Wait until you see the inside." He gave her a friendly wink. "Let's catch up."

She nodded and they walked side by side to the front of the house. "The ramp is well built." It was sturdy beneath her feet, with plenty of space to push and turn nearly two mobility aids side by side.

"The home belonged to a soldier who was severely injured in combat. He built this place from the ground up, and adopted a toddler with quadriplegia." Branch opened the front door and held it for her.

"What happened to them?" She stepped into an open foyer drenched in natural light. Glossy wood floors ran throughout the open-concept living space. They wouldn't need to worry about Jacob's chair getting caught on a rug.

"Met the love of his life, a doctor who had helped place the child with him, and moved across the country."

The tension in her shoulders relaxed. She'd been worried something terrible had happened to them. "I'm glad he moved because of something happy."

"He told the Realtor he wanted the property to go to someone who needed it. Who would make it a happy home."

"That certainly fits Jacob to a T. He spreads sunshine everywhere he goes."

"I've never been around someone like him before, but I'm already glad I'm getting a chance to know him. I've never seen Ransom look so…happy."

She selfishly wanted to be part of the reason for that happiness, which further proved she should get her own apartment and live off-site before things got even more complicated. All she remembered from the night prior was having the reoccurring nightmare. The sickening scent of smoldering flesh. The burn in her lungs as her head was forced in icy salt water until she choked. The snap of bone and the sharp, unstable sensation that followed. Then she was encircled in strong, capable arms and she knew down to her soul that she was safe. She fell asleep with the scent of citrus and bergamot in her nostrils. Something she'd come to associate with comfort and security.

If she gave in to that comfort, though, those lingering gazes and gentle touches, what might happen if things didn't work out? He could fire her, and she'd be out of a job, a place to live, and banned from seeing the child she loved. This morning's conversation didn't inspire much confidence either. While she could emphasize and respect Neo's urge to protect Jacob, it stung that he thought she'd let Jacob get in harm's way. She'd left danger over four thousand miles away in Ireland and years had passed since she'd heard from her brother.

The others were gathered in the kitchen, so they crossed the room to join them. "Look at this." Neo's smile made her heart flip before it steadily resumed beating. "The countertops are mounted. Jacob's chair can slide beneath so he's right up against the ledge."

"That would certainly make hand-over-hand activities easier." The setup was modern and a lot of thought had gone into ensuring ease of use for someone who required daily living assistance. "We can chop vegetables together and you can help me wash dishes."

An exaggerated sigh broke from Jacob's lips. Deep laughter resonated around the room. Even Joker had an amused grin on his face.

"Typical teenager." Brynn shook her head. She loved this side of Jacob's personality—all sass and humor.

They continued around the house, finding more modifications as they went. In the living room, there were tracks for a ceiling hoist that ran down the hall and into the bedroom and one of the bathrooms. Jacob was easy enough to lift now, but someday, when he grew larger, an alternate method to help move him from point A to point B would be a blessing. They followed the ceiling tracks to the first room—a bathroom with a roll-in shower and a jacuzzi tub. There were four bedrooms, including one designed with additional space for turning. The largest room was at the back of the house. Floor-to-ceiling windows faced the backyard and the dense forest surrounding the property. The room opened onto an accessible deck, and the team wasted no time wheeling Jacob outside. A bright orange swing swayed in the summer breeze.

Neo came up beside her. "What are you thinking?"

"That Jacob is going to be sold by that swing." The men already had him up and out of the chair and were pulling the rollercoaster-style harness over his head. "I always look for parks with accessible swings. He loves the sensation of flying through the air."

"I'm sure it's freeing. I want to give him as many opportunities to feel that way as I can." Neo's gaze was fixed on his four brothers as they danced around the swing, taking turns pushing Jacob as high as he could go. With each push, a smile stretched over his face, so wide and bright, a punch of joy flashed to life inside her.

"So what do you think?" Neo angled his body to face her. Touring this home with him brought to mind nights cuddled on the couch—all three of them watching movies. Of summers spent by the pool she'd caught a glimpse of from the kitchen window. Trust was difficult for her, but Neo inspired it, made her want for things meant for others but not herself.

"I think this place probably costs a fortune. Whatever

home you choose, the most important thing is the love within it. The extra amenities and technology will make things easier for sure, but that's not what is most important." She came from a completely different world than Neo. Her mother had knitted blankets and sold them at local tourist markets and her father had been a laborer. They had financial security, but there were no frills. Neo's world, at least the one he'd left behind, was opulence and glitter. Dinner parties and galas. Helicopter rides and custom tailored clothing. That wouldn't typically bother her, and Neo seemed as down to earth as they came, but she didn't know how he couldn't be affected by the world he grew up in.

"I've been careful about spending and investing. I had my own trust fund, set aside from my grandparents, and I haven't touched it. Plus, I have my own money from the service, much less but there all the same. Maybe I didn't know it at a time, but this is what I've been waiting for—the opportunity to use the money I've saved for something important. Family. I never thought I would have one, but now that Jacob's in my life I will do anything to protect him and make sure he has everything he needs. That means you, too, Brynn."

The weight of his hand on her shoulder made her want to lean into the strength of his touch.

"If we bought this house, this would be your room."

Neo had already accepted her into the fold. Started saying dangerous words like *we* and *us* that sent her mind racing with unlikely possibilities that she shouldn't dare to entertain. Her words bottled up in her throat. She wished her nana was still here to help guide her through her confusing feelings. She loved Jacob like a son. Maybe she was just enthralled with Neo because he would be such an important part of Jacob's life. Because she'd always longed for a family that loved and accepted her. When she didn't respond, Neo continued. "There's an en suite attached, so you'll have your privacy, but I hope you'll decide to spend time with us all the same."

She cleared her throat and nearly choked on her words. Ones that were the safest and most practical choice. "I've been thinking that maybe it might be best for me to find a place off-site."

"What do you mean?" He turned to fully face her. "What made you change your mind? Was it our conversation this morning?"

"No. At least, not completely. I think some space between us would be best." Even though she'd only known Neo for a short time, the words made her want to cry. She'd never be whole enough to have a long-term relationship, and trying would only mess up the best thing in her life—Jacob. The realization hit hard. She'd gotten caught up in a silly romantic fantasy where she, Neo, and Jacob were a family. Dreams like that only led to heartbreak.

"If I've done anything to make you uncomfortable, tell me and I'll fix it. You're as much a part of Jacob's life as anyone. I can modify whatever to meet your needs. If you want your own access to the house, I can add a door with a separate lock and key to this room, so you can come in and out as you please. If you need more time for yourself, more days off, I get it and we'll make it work."

"No, Neo. This is nothing to do with you." *And every-*

thing to do with you. "You didn't do anything except offer Jacob the world and get us out of a terrible situation. You've offered kindness." She took a quick breath, needed to finish what was on her mind before she chickened out. "I don't want to get used to relying on you, because that would be hard to lose. I'm not immune to the good man you are. You might see yourself as cold, but you've offered us nothing but warmth. It's better if I stay objective and put space between us. I came here for Jacob, and I don't want to complicate things with the emotions I'm starting to feel for you." She sighed and blinked rapidly. There was a burn of frustration, of vulnerability behind her lids. "That's hard to admit, but you've been honest with me from the start, and I owe you no less in return."

He took a step closer to her, invading her space. His palms touched lightly on her arms. "Thank you for being honest with me. That's something I wanted to talk to you about, in addition to what happened last night. Holding you against me felt so fucking right. It's the first time I've ever done that—held a woman while she slept. Deep in my gut I know I want to see where that can go." He stepped closer, and dropped his forehead to hears. "I'm not gonna pressure you into anything, but I want you to know those feelings aren't one-sided. I know you're here for Jacob, and I would never do anything to isolate you from him, even if things didn't work. We have a spark, though. One that I don't want to ignore."

Now his hands were running up and down her arms and he'd moved back a fraction, his eyes glued to hers. She found her own reflection mirrored in the green depths, could see the spark of desperate hope in her eyes. She licked her lips involuntarily, and Neo's gaze dropped to her mouth.

"I don't want to do anything to hurt Jacob." Her reply fell flat. She was aware that Neo would never hurt her or his brother, no matter how badly things ended.

"Brynn, I want a chance to get to know you as a woman, not just Jacob's nurse. It's fast—I get that. We've only known each other for a short time, but if you've lived like I have, seen how fleeting life can be, you know to reach out and grab the good when you see it. I want you to be under the same roof as us, to spend time together, both as the three of us and time with just me and you. Please, Brynn. Give it a shot, at least for a couple weeks, and if you still feel the same way, I will personally help you find a condo or home nearby."

She took one breath then two. Just this morning, Neo had been questioning whether or not she'd gotten into some kind of trouble that she was now running from. It hit too close to home. Not being believed. The betrayal of her loved ones had etched a jagged scar of mistrust and insecurity down the length of her soul. *Don't let the actions of your parents and brother ruin you, sweet girl. Feel with your heart and soul.* Words she'd long forgotten bubbled back to the surface. Her nana rocking her after she'd tended the wounds inflicted by her brother. She filled her lungs. "I'll think about it." That was the best she could offer right now.

He tucked a strand of her hair behind her ear. "Thank you." His breath tickled her cheek as he moved in closer and pressed his lips to her skin. A tingle shot through her at the simple contact. What would happen when his lips came to hers? *If.* Just because they'd admitted mutual attraction didn't mean she should get ahead of herself and dream of promises and plans. "Come on." His rough voice was deeper, like tires over gravel. "Let's go outside before the guys decide to try out the pool, too." He dropped his hands, breaking the connection between them. She immediately felt the loss of his touch and craved more. As if sensing her disappointment, he squeezed her hand, then released it before pulling open the sliding glass door. The sunshine cascading over the deck warmed her, but not as much as Neo's words had. The second they stepped outside, Joker came striding toward them with a hard look on his face. "Need to talk to you." His gaze cut to her, then back to Neo. "Alone."

"Now?" Neo narrowed his eyes at Joker.

"It's important."

Neo's chin dipped. "Fine."

Brynn was already skirting around them. "I'll see how Jacob is doing." Unease prickled her skin. Joker's glare had been meant for her alone, and the earlier conversation with Neo played over in her mind. Had Neo asked Joker to look into her? Or was he just voicing his general displeasure of having her around? Maybe it had nothing to do with her at all, but her stomach twisted all the same.

CHAPTER ELEVEN

NEO STOOD AT the stove and used tongs to flip the browning chicken. Despite what Joker had told him this afternoon, he couldn't help but grin at the singing coming from the bathroom of his apartment. Like the first night he laid eyes on Brynn, she was crooning an off-key version of a Miley Cyrus song, and Jacob was busting a gut. He'd learned that his brother loved pop music and being in the water. He enjoyed foot massages and scrambled eggs, but hated being tickled and eating broccoli. Brynn had showed him twice now how to puree Jacob's food so he could safely eat it and how to use a pestle and mortar to grind his medications so they could be flushed through his feeding tube without having the line clog. They had gotten so lucky to tour a home specifically designed for a child with special needs. It was as though the home was custom-made for them. Kind of like Jacob and Brynn seemed like a made-to-order family that fit like a puzzle piece into his life.

The moment they got into the car after touring the home, he called the Realtor to submit an offer above the asking price. He didn't want to take any chances with the property that would be their new home. The Realtor had also called the previous owner to explain Jacob's needs and how well the house fit his medical challenges. They could start moving in immediately if the offer was accepted, and he'd list his apartment. He wanted to make sure Jacob and Brynn were settled before he got called out on another mission. Every day, the situation in the Middle East was brewing, and he knew it was only a matter of time before they got the call for wheels up.

He didn't want to waste any time getting to know Brynn in case they were called out sooner rather than later. Plus, he needed to talk to her about Joker. A conversation he was not looking forward to having. Joker was trying to protect him, but he was still pissed that his teammate had gone behind his back and run an in-depth search on Brynn's past. Only one thing had stood out—a police report filed by a family member to investigate abuse within the home. The police department had stated Brynn was known to make up lies about her sibling, and suggested she seek counseling.

He wanted some time alone with her to discuss what Joker had done. Brynn was going to be hurt, and that plain sucked. He'd apologize on his teammate's behalf, but he also needed answers. Someone in her hometown wanted to shut down a potential investigation into her brother's actions. Despite his general mistrust, he'd experienced Brynn quaking in his arms. That fear wasn't imagined or acted. Perhaps she'd reported being abused by a sibling, too, only to be brushed off. It would explain why she was always trying to do the right thing, why trust was hard for her.

They'd given Jacob an early dinner, and Neo was fixing something special for the two of them. He got the feeling Brynn rarely relaxed, and he wanted to put her at ease to talk about the words they'd exchanged that afternoon and what

Joker had discovered. He was humbled and thrilled that she was developing feelings for him and trusted him enough to admit it. Everything about Brynn was real and raw, from the emotions she wore so plainly on her face to how she belted out a tune, not caring how it sounded. He wanted her to take a chance and stay with him and Jacob in the new house. He hadn't had many things in his life that were soft, kind, and beautiful, but when he saw Brynn, he found all those things and more. He might be out of his mind, but he was prepared to do whatever it took to keep her long-term. He was going to keep that sentiment to himself for now because he didn't want to scare her off.

He was draining the pasta when he heard soft footsteps padding along the floor. Her midnight hair was loose around her shoulders. Her delicate features content but sleepy.

"He's asleep. The day must've worn him out." She absently ran her fingers through her hair, highlighting the gloss that seemed to coat every tendril. "What can I help you with?"

"After insisting on putting Jacob to bed, which involved lifting him in and out of the bathtub, getting him dressed and medicated, you're asking to help? Sit down, woman. Let someone else take care of you for a change." Instead of falling boneless to the couch like he expected, she perched on one of the barstools at the small center island.

He took a glass, filled it halfway from the bottle breathing on the counter, and grabbed a Sprite from the refrigerator. "You can tell me how this wine is," he said, placing a glass in front of her. "And if you don't like it, Old Faithful is right here." He put the soda on the counter next to her wineglass.

She blushed and dipped her chin. There was far too much appreciation in her eyes for a glass of wine and a can of soda. Made him want to spoil her rotten. "Thank you. I feel totally useless, you know." She took a sip and closed her eyes.

The relaxation on her face made something click inside of him. He enjoyed taking care of her and hoped to make it a habit. When they left the house tour, he'd quickly stopped at the grocery store and purchased what he needed to make chicken piccata. It was one of his favorites growing up because his grandfather actually made it, not their personal chef. It was something that he'd taught Neo how to cook, and to this day, it was probably the only thing he made that was half decent. He'd also grabbed some toast points at the store and cheated with premade bruschetta. Neo put the appetizer in front of Brynn on the small island, where they could talk as he finished putting the meal together.

"You know, drinking and stuffing my face is not helping." She laughed. "That's me lounging on my butt while you do all the work."

"You don't do nearly enough lounging from where I'm sitting." He shot her a pointed look over his shoulder. "It's my pleasure to cook for you, although I can't guarantee your stomach will feel the same way."

Brynn chuckled. He loved how the sound echoed through the kitchen. "Is that your disclaimer? Eating Neo's cooking may result in foodborne illness?"

"Maybe. Consume at your own risk," he teased. His cheeks hurt from smiling so much, something he'd been doing a lot of the past few days. Suddenly, he had a purpose outside the Teams, which felt good. He was constantly ramping up for the next mission, never having a life outside of being a SEAL. He was enjoying himself in a way he never had. Cooking dinner for a woman was another first. He always made sure the women he took to bed knew the score. Knew that he wasn't looking for strings or a relationship. The bar scene had gotten old, though, and it had been a long time since he lost himself in meaningless pleasure. If he made love to Brynn, it would be a totally different experience. The last thing he wanted was for her to think that he was lusting after her because she was a convenient option due to their close proximity. She needed to know, without a doubt, he wanted more than just that gorgeous body.

"Okay, then, if you insist. I will sit right here and enjoy the wine and the food. And maybe the view, too."

He looked over his shoulder and stood a little straighter because of her words. It was the first time Brynn had outright flirted with him, and the intense blush on her face indicated that she was surprised by what she'd said. Like the words had just slipped from her mouth.

"I'm happy to provide dinner and a show, sweetheart." He turned to the stove and plated the chicken and pasta before joining her at the bar. He sat at the corner so he could face her as they ate.

"This looks and smells delicious." She inhaled the scent of the food. "Might even be worth some food poisoning." She cut into her chicken and took a bite, a deep sigh tumbling from her lips. "This is amazing," she said, covering her full mouth. Her simple enjoyment made him feel ten feet tall. He'd cook for her every day for that kind of reaction.

He'd put extra effort into the meal, and it was paying off. Every little sigh and moan of pleasure made him wonder if she would make the same sounds when he was deep inside her. He was pleased when she cleared her plate, eating every last bite. Money had been tight for her because of his mother, and she'd probably given up far too many meals to support Jacob. He stood and took their plates to the sink, quickly rinsing them and bringing the bottle of wine over to the center island.

"Can I top you off?"

"Are you trying to get me drunk so I spill all my secrets?" She was attempting to joke, but the sadness beneath her tone made him step closer and push back her hair. He couldn't seem to stop himself from touching it. Now wasn't the time to think about fisting his hands in it and kissing the hell out of her, but damn if the image didn't cross his mind. They needed to get some things out in the open before anything physical was even on the table.

"Whatever works, as long as you know your secrets are safe with me."

"I know that, or I wouldn't be open to sharing anything at all. It's not something I like to relive, but if we are going to live within the same walls, you should know some of my history. It's not uncommon for me to have those nightmares, although I had no idea I screamed in my sleep. Now I wonder how often I disturb Jacob or concern him during the night."

He held out his hand, palm up. "Let's talk in the living room." She placed her hand in his and slid off the stool.

"I'm programmed to be aware and alert." They walked

over to the couch. Brynn sat in the middle, curling her feet beneath her like a cat. "Even during rest. It's possible that Jacob never woke up or heard a thing. Even the slightest noise will wake me from a deep sleep."

"And you still want me to stay in the same home? I can't guarantee I won't wake you up, and your job is dangerous. Sleep is important."

"If you have a nightmare," he said, taking her smooth hand back in his own, "I want to hear it, Brynn. Maybe it's too soon to sleep in the same bed, but if you're scared, I want to hold you like I did last night. I want you to feel safe and protected even when I'm not around. As soon as the offer is accepted on the house, I will install a security system, so you feel secure when I'm on missions. I won't be able to tell you where I am or how long I'll be gone, but know I'm doing everything I can to get back in one piece."

Her face sobered. Shit. Maybe he shouldn't put the thought that he could be maimed or killed into her head. Still, she deserved to know what she was getting into if she took a chance on him. Once he told her what Joker had done, she might not want to be under the same roof at all.

"Listen, Brynn. I have to tell you something. It's not something I asked for. Certainly not something I'm happy about. Actually, it pissed me right the fuck off. Joker looked into your past, and he looked deep." He held his breath, waiting for her reaction. It was a violation for sure, and he'd thoroughly reamed out Joker for making that call behind his back.

Brynn's expression blanked. "That's what he wanted to talk to you about at the home tour this afternoon. The thing that couldn't wait."

"Yes," he answered, and Brynn removed her hand from his, tucking her arms around her waist. Hell. She was putting physical distance between them already, and he couldn't blame her one bit.

"Well?" Her voice was so quiet, it nearly was lost in the low hum of the central air-conditioning unit.

"He told me about the police report. Why did it get shoved under the rug? Why would the police think you were making that up?" Again, the breath bottled in his chest as he waited for her response. He didn't give a damn what the report said. Brynn was honest by nature.

She seemed to fold into herself, distress and sadness pulsing around her, so thick it was palpable. "That's why I stopped telling. No one could see past my brother's façade. He was the football captain. So smart he was the top of his class. Charming, too. Well-liked. He was going to be something. I was nothing special—an average student, with unremarkable traits, not popular like Fergus."

Her words pissed him off. He wanted to be the person to show her how remarkable she really was. "Joker said a family member reported the abuse."

She nodded. "My nana did. I had told a teacher once, too, and my parents a couple of years before that." Her chin dipped, and with it, his heart. He wanted to wrap her up and protect her from the memories, but he had to know. His brother's safety might depend on it.

"Shit. Brynn, I'm so sorry."

She looked up, and her eyes were wide. "I haven't even told you what happened, but it sounds like..." She let the words trail off and glanced down.

"What, Brynn?" he encouraged.

"Like you believe it happened." Her gaze raised up, and what he found there nearly gutted him. Unshed tears pooled along her lower lids, but behind the glassy surface there was a hint of hope.

"Because I do. I might not know the little things about you like your favorite color, but I know enough. I know you love Sprite and ugly dogs. You've got a sweet tooth and you're honest...so much that you'd think of returning a library book when your world has been turned upside down. You were willing to go without pay and take responsibility for my brother, and sell all of your things to make it work. You make him laugh and give him the dignity and respect he deserves. You open your heart to strangers experiencing the same journey and offer them a shoulder to lean on. So yeah, I might not know the details of what happened, but I know enough about you, about the stuff that's important, to know I believe you. And Brynn?"

"Yeah?" she croaked out, tears now freely streaming down her face.

"There is not one thing average or unremarkable about you." There was a tremor in her hunched shoulders. In the time he'd known her, she stood straight and strong. It physically hurt to witness her pain. "Will you tell me what happened?" he said, changing the subject. "When did it start?"

Brynn withdrew into herself again, curling up even tighter as though the memories would swallow her up. This time, though, she unwound her arms from her waist and sought his touch, slipping her hand into his. Made him feel even worse that Joker had stumbled upon an event so traumatic it had rocked her young world.

"I mentioned that I grew up in Ireland." Her voice was quiet, almost fragile. "That my grandmother traveled to the United States with me. It wasn't some grand adventure. It was an escape." She paused and took a few breaths. Tension swirled within him, tightening and pulsing beneath his skin. What the hell had she been through? "Since the moment I was born, my brother hated me. I know that because I bear scars I don't even remember receiving. Old ones. He had been the only child and the sole recipient of my parents' affection. Like I said, Fergus was gifted in many ways. He had a talent for numbers, and his teachers loved him. He was studious and always said the right things to adults around us. Money wasn't tight, but it wasn't abundant either. Fergus took the opportunity to strike when my parents were at work or preoccupied with other things."

She went silent as if choosing her words carefully. He gave her the time she needed, even though possible scenarios were racing through his head, each worse than the last. His skin was crawling with the need to pull her into his arms, but he stayed rooted in place. She might be unable to make it through what she was about to say with him holding her.

Brynn shifted uncomfortably. "He took great pleasure in telling me how he tortured and killed small animals, but I stupidly believed that he'd made those stories up to taunt and frighten me. I knew he was telling the truth when he began to turn the torture on me." She took a shuddery breath, and his free hand curled into a tight fist of rage. He tucked it into the pocket of his sweats, so he didn't scare her.

"How old were you when the abuse began?" His voice was coated in darkness. Cold and hard. It was the voice his teammates and enemies were used to hearing.

"The first time I remember Fergus hurting me, I was around seven. The day before, Fergus said he had a secret surprise that he wanted to show me. I didn't want to go with him, but he was babysitting, so I didn't have a choice. He walked me down to a cave along the shoreline where he kept his projects. Inside, he made me look at every single mutilated dead animal that had the misfortune of falling into his hands. Kittens. Shrews. Hedgehogs. It was clear he did all sorts of sick experiments in that cave. That night, I told my parents about what I'd seen. They didn't believe me, though. They told me to stop telling stories."

"Shit, Brynn. Please tell me they looked in that cave."

"I begged them to let me show them the location. It was so close to the house, but they refused to feed into my little tantrum. They said even if it were true, boys will be boys. It was the same at school. No one could believe the smartest, most popular student at school could do anything wrong. Fergus found out that I had told my teacher and said I was the next animal that was going to end up in his cave." She was breathing hard, hands trembling in her lap.

"Take your time, sweetheart. Can't be easy to talk about but I'm damn proud of you." He flexed and fisted his hand repeatedly inside his pocket, fighting for calm, even while holding her other hand gently in his. She nodded, eyes glassy and clouded with fear.

"He dragged me down the slope and back among his

projects. I must have lost consciousness when he slammed me into the rocks because when I woke up, he was gone. My pants were around my ankles. The word *liar* was carved into my thigh. I stumbled up the cliffs, fighting to get back home. Fergus and my parents sat at the kitchen table eating dinner like their seven-year-old hadn't been missing in the middle of a storm. My parents grounded me for staying out past dark. I tried to tell them what happened, but they said my lies were getting concerning. I tried to show them the word on my leg, but my mother slapped me and told me to go upstairs and stay in my room for the rest of the night. Typically, I went to the market with my mother on Sundays to help her sell her blankets, but Fergus had to watch me because I was grounded. I tried once more to tell a teacher, but Fergus broke three of my toes. I didn't tell on him after that. I should've told Nana what was going on to start with, but after the teachers and my own parents didn't believe me, I thought she would have no reason to either. It wasn't until years later that she noticed one of my scars and demanded to know what had happened. After that, she confronted my parents and Fergus, but they still denied it. Fergus was their golden child. They refused to do anything about the situation, so Nana packed me up, and we flew to the United States. She saved my life. I'm sure of it. The abuse was getting worse and worse, and I didn't know how to defend myself. I was twelve then. If I fought back, he hurt me tenfold or made up lies to spread around the schoolyard trying to discredit me."

"Jesus, Brynn." His jaw was clenched in anger toward her sorry excuse for parents. Nearly as much as the older brother who should've protected her but repeatedly assaulted her. He wanted to fly across the country and throttle the twisted bastard. Wanted to rage at her parents for choosing one child over the other. He was an asshole for thinking he had a rough childhood. He was neglected, sure, and left alone most of the time, but no one was there to beat him or torture him. How Brynn was sitting in front of him, had made something of herself, was a miracle. And the fact that she chose a career helping and nurturing others? A testament to her unbreakable spirit. The respect he had for her, which was already high, kicked up another notch. This woman might look delicate, but she continued to prove she had a spine of steel.

"I'm so damn sorry, Brynn. Sorry that no one stepped up and looked into the allegations against Fergus. I hate your parents for letting him get away with hurting you. Your grandmother did what every person before her should've done and whisked you away so no one could hurt you. Please tell me you eventually got some justice? That Fergus had to pay for his crimes."

Her long hair swayed as she shook her head. "No, the last time I saw him, he held my head in a bucket of ice water. Later that afternoon, my grandmother visited and noticed I was lethargic. She demanded to know what had happened. Then I showed her what he carved into my legs so many years before and the burn marks and lacerations on my body."

"How could your parents deny something so visible?" Hostility welled up inside him at the hurt and fear that the child Brynn once was had endured such terror.

"They said I must've done it myself to spite Fergus. To make him look guilty. It hurt nearly as bad as the abuse that they would reject me so easily. That they didn't believe my words. My grandmother saved my life that day. I'm sure of it. I don't know how much longer I would've survived. As far as I know, Fergus went on living as he had been. The golden child playing his sick games. Nana reported him to the local police, but I don't know what came of it if anything."

He sat silently for a moment, trying to gather his frayed edges and lock his emotions down, so he didn't frighten her. "You would've survived. I have no doubt you would've found another way to escape, but I'm glad that someone stepped up for you and had your back. I wish I could've met your grandmother. She sounds almost as strong as her granddaughter. You amaze me, Brynn. I know a lot of hard-ass SEALs who would've cracked under similar pressure, yet you're brave enough to be as kind and good as you are." He reached for her now, pulling her onto his lap and encircling her with his arms. "I am in awe of you." He whispered into her ear, and her head fell against his shoulder. Her shuddery breaths rocked in and out against his chest.

"Sometimes, my brain tricks me and I'm still in Ireland. Waking up, not knowing what the day will hold. What kind of horrors Fergus will have in store for me."

"He's not here, though. I will never let anyone put a finger on you. You are safe here and I will protect you with everything I am." He meant every word. He'd gladly die before Brynn experienced more pain. Knew she would care for Jacob like her own. Neo would use every resource at his disposal to ensure Fergus was still in Ireland and that somebody seriously looked into his crimes. Torturing animals and his own sister spoke volumes about the type of person he might be now if you could call him human. No, Fergus was a monster hiding beneath a sheath of skin. He'd seen the type over and over again. If Fergus was still alive, he'd bet every penny he owned that the man was now a serial killer.

He'd never been gladder to be a SEAL. To have the skills and the network of contacts necessary to protect Brynn. He vowed to keep her safe. He was more than a little apprehensive now about leaving for a mission. He'd keep his fingers crossed to move them into the new house before they left. Security had been on his to-do list before, but now it was essential.

"What triggers the nightmares?" he asked. She had melted into him, and he wasn't sure she was still awake until she cleared her throat.

"The morning in the hotel, I saw someone with his likeness and panicked. When I looked back, though, the person was gone. Sometimes stress makes my brain do funny things, and I think I see him from the corner of my eye. Crazy, huh?"

"Not at all." Fuck. He did not like the sounds of that. Not one fucking bit. Brynn had been told her whole childhood she was a liar. Would she really believe herself if she actually saw Fergus in public?

"Thank you for trusting me with this. I'm so sorry for everything you went through, and I wish I could change it, but I am not sorry your grandmother brought you to the United States or that you're in my life because of it." He smoothed his hands down her hair. So beautiful and brave. "It's been a long day, and you didn't sleep well last night. Let's get you into bed. Thank you again for sharing your secret with me. You never have to hide from me. Ever."

He considered climbing into bed beside Brynn, wanting the reassurance that she was okay and safe, but instead, he kissed her on the forehead and returned to his bedroom. There were other ways to protect her, and he needed to ensure her physical safety before anything.

He sent a group text to his team to set up a meeting the next day. Brynn was his to protect, and he wanted to know exactly what he was up against. His teammates and commander needed to know if Fergus would be a threat. A foolproof way to track the bastard brother was the only thing that would calm the anguish in his soul. Maybe Fergus had forgotten all about Brynn, but he didn't think so. He'd seen evil before, and evil rarely stopped once it had sunken its teeth into something so pure and innocent.

CHAPTER TWELVE

Brynn reread the note Neo had left on the kitchen table. Wetness trickled down her cheeks, but she swiped it away. He'd filled her tea kettle with water so she could start it as soon as she woke up, replenished the bagels and cream cheese she preferred, and left her a copy of the key to the apartment. No man had ever treated her with such care and respect. He wrote that he had an emergency meeting with his team but would be home by noon. Recounting the events from her childhood hadn't been easy, and today she felt vulnerable and raw. She couldn't deny her disappointment when Neo hadn't climbed into bed beside her, but there were still so many misgivings about their attraction. The risk of having a physical relationship with him was so huge, and yet, she couldn't stop thinking about him.

She couldn't express how badly she longed to fall into a dreamless sleep with his strong arms locked around her and his scent in the air. Of course, she was being silly, letting her infatuation with him get the best of her. After all, she had thought about moving into another space, and Neo had done his best to convince her otherwise. She wanted to stay. She was just afraid of her own feelings. She'd been on her own for a long time, and it wasn't Neo's duty to make her feel safe. Just having him in the same house eased some of her anxiety. Fergus was a long way away and couldn't hurt her anymore. Besides, she had a lot to be thankful for. Aside from Jacob, this was the first time since Nana died that she'd had good people in her life. People who cared about her well-being.

Jacob was sitting with his eyes closed and his face tilted up to the sun streaming through the windows. He'd just finished some oatmeal, making it clear that was not his preferred breakfast, and was now listening to music. It was a glorious summer day, still cool enough to spend some time outdoors.

"What do you say about going for a walk? Exploring the area a little? We could walk by the public school, which would be the same whether we stayed in this apartment or moved into the new home we saw yesterday. I set up a meeting with your teacher and aide later this week."

Jacob turned his head at the mention of school. It had been so hard to dismiss him from his middle school in Boston. One of the highlights of his day was getting picked up by the bus in the morning and seeing his friends. He was naturally social despite being nonverbal, and his dramatic expressions made it easy to decipher Jacob's feelings and choices. They explored all different types of devices to help Jacob communicate, but the easiest way remained looking at his face and nonverbal cues. After applying his sunscreen and putting a baseball cap on his head, she wheeled Jacob to the apartment door. She took the elevator to the lobby level. She was still shaken up after recalling her childhood trauma but refused to stay inside and wallow.

They stepped outside onto the brick walkway, and the

scent of sea salt and brine overpowered her senses. She'd gotten her first glimpse of how close Neo lived to the ocean yesterday. This beach was nothing like the craggy rocks and violent waves of her home in Ireland, but one with miles of smooth golden sand, striped umbrellas, and wooden piers. They walked past local restaurants and shops, stopping every so often to peer at an intricate window display. An outdoor vendor was selling bumper stickers, and she slowed down to read some of the sayings.

"Look, Jacob, this one says, *Proud Brother of a United States Sailor.*" The Navy's crest appeared in the middle.

Jacob smiled and let out a pleased sigh.

"I'll get it, and we can put it on your chair." She paid the vendor for the sticker and found a quiet spot along the road. "Do you want this on the side of your chair or the back? You let me know." She paused and then asked, "The side?" She gave him several seconds to respond, and when he didn't, she said, "The back?" Jacob immediately turned his head.

"The back of the chair it is." She peeled off the film on the back of the sticker and carefully smoothed out the vinyl.

Before they continued walking, she pulled up a map on her phone. "Looks like if we keep heading in this general direction, the school is only a few blocks away." They passed a brick building painted with a mural of the ocean and a surfer riding the waves in bold blue and canary yellow. Jacob seemed fascinated, so they stopped and looked at it for a while before heading on.

It was undoubtedly a military town because everywhere they walked, she saw men and women in uniform. She was sure Neo looked incredibly handsome in his, although she wasn't sure what a SEAL actually wore. With his broad shoulders and a powerful back, he'd be a mouthwatering sight in anything at all. He had defined arms and muscular, thick thighs. She could feel the toned muscle corded beneath her when he'd held her in his lap last night. "So far, I really like Virginia. I wasn't sure about the move, but I'm glad we came. Are you happy here?"

She couldn't see Jacob's face as she pushed him, but his head turned, and the high curve of his cheek told her he was grinning. As they walked inland, the smaller shops became sparse, replaced by historic residential buildings constructed of brick. The sidewalk was shaded by the canopy of towering sycamores, and black cherry bushes hung ripe with fruit. Showy pink and white magnolia blossoms hung from glossy green leaves, permeating the air with their sweet floral fragrance. According to her map, they were nearly at the school.

Movement to the left caught her eye. She turned, but no one was there. An uneasy feeling skated down her spine. She took a calming breath and continued on. The whole reason they were on this walk was to visit the school; she wasn't going to let her paranoia deter them. Cold hit her chest as they continued to move forward, as though every cell in her body was telling her to turn back. There was a rustle in trees across the street, and she halted in her tracks.

"Jacob, I'm so sorry. We need to turn back. We're in an unfamiliar place, and I'm starting to feel anxious. It's almost noon, and we can ask Neo if he'd drive by the school with us. Maybe he even has some news on the house." She scanned the area and turned; the sensation of being watched filled her with dread. Maybe it hadn't been wise to go over her trauma in such detail. She was in a new place with new people; if she tried, she could find fictional danger in every corner. She was suddenly aware of her heartbeat, racing and pounding in her chest. She glanced over her shoulder—still nothing. A branch cracked behind her, but she refused to look. She pushed Jacob faster until she was in a full-blown run. Typically Jacob would be laughing. But he wasn't laughing right now.

He was good at reading people and could sense her heightened anxiety. Maybe she was being irrational, but the sudden urge to get away and back into the safety of the apartment was too strong to ignore. When she heard her name, she pushed faster. Her brain was tricking her, making her hear someone thousands of miles away. Knowing that she was on the verge of a panic attack did nothing to ease the sensation of danger. She didn't slow even when her lungs began to burn.

She could hear someone scuttling along behind her and glanced over her shoulder. Her foot caught on an uneven brick and she came down hard. She grabbed the rim of Jacob's chair to stop his forward momentum, banging her face against the ground. There was pressure on her back, and she scrambled forward to escape. She turned, shielding her face to protect herself, when something wet lapped across her cheek. A large dog towered over her. She couldn't get a good look at it with its stout nose and bullish jowls so close to her face. The animal whimpered, then plopped down on top of her. Relief flooded through her, clouding her eyes with tears. On a long, shaky breath, she sat up, wiggling out from under the weight of the dog. The crazy thing was wagging its tail like it had just found the world's biggest Milk-Bone. It could use a whole box of them and a few months' worth of decent meals. While the dog's head was massive, its body was rail-thin to the point it looked almost unsteady on spindly legs.

"I'm so glad it was you chasing me. I feel like a total idiot," she muttered, running a hand over the dog's head. Its coat was so filthy it was hard to tell what color it was. Maybe a light brown or gray. The dog attempted to lap the blood off her hands, but she pulled away. "I'm okay, Jacob," she called up to him. "But I hope Neo isn't allergic to animals. I think we just found ourselves a tagalong."

The dog walked with a limp to the front of the chair as she struggled to her feet on unsteady legs. Jacob was cackling with a fervor she'd never heard before as the dog nudged his hands and put a paw on his lap. "Well, now that you've caught up to us, we better start walking. I need to get cleaned up." Blood was seeping from the cut on her knee, soaking her jeans and dripping from her lips. She kept wiping it away from her chin with the back of her hand. The dog walked at Jacob's side, its ginger gait becoming more pronounced with each step. They continued past the shops and restaurants until the apartment came into view.

She wasn't sure about the dog policy, but there was no way she would leave the animal on its own, especially after it walked all this way with them. She pressed the assistive door opener and pushed the wheelchair through. The dog followed dutifully behind them, not even backing away when the elevator doors slid open. He walked ahead of them and plopped his bottom on the floor, wagging his tail in exhausted ticks. She pressed the button for Neo's floor. They had taken one step down the hall when Neo's apartment door burst open.

"Oh my God. What happened? Are you okay?" He rushed down the corridor and inspected Jacob before rounding the wheelchair and putting his arm around her. "You're hurt. Bleeding." He took over, pushing the wheelchair with his free hand while guiding her down the hall.

"I thought I heard someone following us, thought I heard my name, and panicked. I started running and tripped only to discover it was actually a dog chasing us. Jacob's fine. He didn't fall." They walked over the threshold and into the apartment. "I couldn't leave the dog outside. He looks to be in such rough shape." For the first time, Neo seemed to notice the animal standing in his kitchen. "He's been nothing but friendly."

"Okay." He eyed the dog suspiciously. "I'm going to get Jacob out of the chair and settled on the couch. Then we'll take a look at those wounds and figure out what to do about the dog. Wait for me in the bathroom, yeah?"

Instead of going to the bathroom, Brynn made her way to her bedroom and rifled through her bag of belongings for her bicycle shorts. Attempting to roll up her straight jeans over her knee was no good, not to mention it would hurt. Part of her was relieved that she had told Neo about her scars the night before. She didn't want to imagine what he'd think when he saw *liar* on her thigh and other old deformities. The other part of her was still hesitant. She wanted Neo to see her as a desirable woman, but how could he see past all of her scars?

Jeans and long pants were her best friends. You'd never catch her in a skirt or dress, and she only wore the shorts when alone with no chance of a visitor. She shut her bedroom door and peeled off her pants, hissing when the rough material rubbed over the new cut. She turned to grab the shorts off the bed and nearly tripped over the dog. For such a massive animal, he moved silently. He must've snuck in the door behind her. The dog tilted its head, and she smiled.

"You're a silly guy, aren't you?" She patted him on the head, and his fur was soft beneath her fingers despite the dirt covering him from head to toe. When she left the bedroom, Neo was already waiting for her.

"Why don't you hop up on the counter, sweetheart?" To his credit, his gaze didn't linger over the scars below her knees. He turned toward the bathroom closet and withdrew a first aid kit. She hoisted herself up, and the dog sat by her dangling feet. Every so often, his wet tongue flicked her ankle in reassurance.

"Looks like you have a new buddy." Even though his tone was carefully controlled, the current beneath rippled with anger. Was it because he'd caught a glimpse of the results of her childhood trauma or something else? Neo opened the case and began laying out packets of antiseptic, ointment, and long Q-tips. His movements were jerky, and his expression tight. "I have some chicken thawed in the fridge. Plain rice in the closet. His stomach won't be able to take much, so a bland diet for a few days would be best." Here was a man who'd seen bloodshed, caused it even, to safeguard people he'd never met. One who was worrying over a sick animal's diet and enraged by decade-old scars.

"Then we can work on transitioning him to real dog food." He tore one of the packets open and pulled out a towelette. "This is for cleaning the wounds."

"You're going to let him stay?" The hope was audible in her voice.

Neo offered a tense smile. "We'll have to do some digging and make sure he's a stray, but I don't hate the idea of a big mutt around when I'm overseas." And there it was again. Neo was a protector to his core, and he'd decided at some point that she fell under his umbrella of fortification. But she didn't want to be thought of as someone he needed to protect. She wanted him to see her as a woman, an equal. Yet, sitting up on the countertop as Neo tended her wounds, she'd never felt more damaged. Embarrassment prickled over her skin, leaving her neck, face, and ears white-hot.

"What was that look?"

"Nothing."

"Don't hide from me."

"Bossy."

"Yep."

"I hate my scars. They make me feel…damaged. Undesirable. Less."

Fury flashed across his face, and he dropped the towelettes, gripping the edge of the counter. "Wanna know what I think of when I see those scars?"

"No." She couldn't bear to know what he thought. Didn't want to see the pity in his eyes.

"Too bad," he bit out, and her gaze snapped up to his. "They make me ballistic on your behalf. Seeing what was done to you makes me fucking irrational. But when I look at those scars, sweetheart, the thing I see most is your grit. Your will to survive. Mystified that you became a nurturer, a healer despite being tortured and rejected by your family. When I think of you, of everything you are, undesirable and damaged don't make the list. Not even fucking close."

Holy shit. All she could manage was a breathless "Oh." He'd just given her words that were cool aloe soothing a blistering sunburn and that was the only thing she could get past the threshold of her lips. Neo tore open the package of a new towel and went to work on another scrape.

"Can I ask you something?" She fidgeted on the stone countertop but stayed in place. If she moved, she'd tumble off. Neo's close proximity was doing funny things to her insides, making her light-headed and breathless. He reached into the cabinet below the sink and returned with a bottle of what appeared to be more antiseptic. Apparently, the towelettes hadn't done the job he'd hoped for.

"Sure." He drenched a loose pad of gauze and pressed the cool material to her knee, gently washing away the dried blood and debris.

"You're a nurturer, too. A healer. You must know that, right?"

"What? No." A deep crease formed between his brows.

"I know you see yourself differently."

"Differently is an understatement. I'm no healer; the opposite—I take lives. Certainly never have been called nurturing."

"You care for everyone around you. And yes, you may have to take lives, but in doing so you save others. You ask for nothing in return." She looked down at her hands before locking them together and returning her gaze. "But what happens if you're hurt on a mission? Or come home exhausted and could use help getting your groceries and things? Who keeps an eye out for you while you're off saving the world?" She took an overdue breath and tugged at her bottom lip with her teeth. She hadn't meant to go off on a tangent, but really, the man didn't expect enough from others, it seemed.

He stiffened, the red-tinged gauze still clenched in his hand. He tossed it in the bathroom trash, and just when she'd given up hope of getting an answer, he cleared his throat. "You're the first person to ever ask me that. To be concerned about my safety." His voice had gone gruff again, making her ache in places she had no business thinking of when it came to Neo. "But the answer is no one. In the Teams, we have each other's backs, even when we're back in the US, but I have a feeling the kind of care you're talking about and the kind I'm used to are two different things."

"Now you have Jacob and me. It's not just a one-way street, Neo. You can lean on us. We'll think of you while you're gone and be here waiting when you come home." Sudden emotion jammed into the base of her throat. When he was gone, she'd be worried about him, scared for him, but despite their lack of time together, she'd miss their closeness, too. And that was the part that frightened her the most. That she was coming to depend on Neo for adult companionship, not to mention developing the mother of all crushes on a man she barely knew.

"It's going to be that much harder to leave, but I can't deny knowing you and Jacob are here, safe and happy, and will be waiting on me doesn't feel good." His voice was choked, and he cleared his throat before asking, "Are you sure it was just the dog out there?"

"I—I had asked Jacob if he'd like to stroll past the school and he was excited. I pulled the directions up on my phone and thought we could walk because it was such a nice day. When we made our way out of the downtown area, I heard footsteps behind me, but when I turned, no one was there. Then I thought I heard my name." She exhaled. "I guess I just kind of panicked. I felt like someone was watching me and started to get that tightness in my chest like I was going to have a panic attack. I kept hearing rustling, but when I turned around, nothing was there. I started running, but I was distracted by fear and fell. That's when the dog came out of hiding. You must think I'm nuts."

"No." The single word held more ferocity than she'd ever heard. "I think you're a woman who's been through a hell of a lot, and is smart to stay alert and wary of her surroundings. I would've gotten out of there if I thought someone was following me, too."

"Even though I feel silly, I'm glad there was no real danger, just a dog looking for help. I hope you're not upset that I brought him into the apartment, but look at him." She gestured toward the dog, who was lying down on the bath mat, staring at her reverently.

"I am not upset. After these cuts are cleaned, I'll fill a warm bath, and we can soap the dog up and see what we're working with. He might have wounds that need attention."

"Do you think someone's looking for him?" She released a long breath.

"I don't know. It's possible."

Neo dressed her wounds with care, cleaned the cuts with antiseptic, and carefully put gauze and medical tape over her knee. He cleaned the more minor scratches on her hands and covered them with ointment.

"No lifting tonight, especially with the condition of your hands. I'll talk to the commander about getting an additional few days off if they're not healed by the time I'm supposed to return on duty."

"They'll be fine now. I've had worse." The moment she said the words, she wanted to retract them.

He braced his hands on either side of the counter, just beyond her outer thighs, and dropped his head. The muscles of his back flexed and retracted with each heavy breath. He was fighting for calm, but the cold fury radiated off of him in waves, cording the tendons of his neck and arms. His reaction on her behalf, just like the way he'd believed her story, healed another piece of her splintered heart.

"Sorry, that was a stupid thing for me to say." Her quiet words didn't seem to reach him. It was like he'd momentarily forgotten she was there. Trying to comfort him, she ran her fingers over his temples, tracing down toward his cheekbones. She liked how his short hair prickled her fingers, and the soft skin of his cheeks was balanced by the chiseled bone beneath. He leaned into her touch but didn't look up.

"I hate that you went through that. Alone. A fucking child." He reached up and placed his hand over hers. He straightened, kissing her palm, then her forehead. Warmth spread through her chest at the affectionate gesture. Even though he seemed calmer, his breathing had grown harder.

He leveled his gaze, and she took a quick gulp of air. His pupils were blown out, black eclipsing the green, and the heat swirling there made her nipples harden beneath her shirt. He was standing between her thighs, and she placed her hands on his chest.

She inadvertently swept her tongue over her lips, and with a tortured groan, he dropped his gaze. The small gap between them held an electric charge that was nearly magnetic. She felt inexplicably drawn to him. Finally, he gave in to whatever internal battle he was warring with and crashed over her. His mouth met hers, tongue licking the seam of her lips. She immediately parted for him, and he consumed. Devoured. Need slammed into her gut, turning her insides liquid. His hands were in her hair, angling her head so he could take her mouth deeply. His tongue clashed with hers in a dance that had wetness pooling between her thighs. She'd never experienced anything this intense, and it was merely a kiss. His taste was peppermint and coffee, with something else that was all his own. Everything around them faded, except for the knowledge that she didn't want this to stop.

His hands released her hair and skimmed down her back. Cupping her from behind, he slid her flush against him, so the result of his attraction was hard against her core. He swallowed the moans tumbling from somewhere deep within her. She gripped his shirt, drunk on the taste and feel of him. She was moments from wrapping her legs around his waist when he pulled back, chest heaving.

"Fuck, Brynn." He rested his forehead against hers, waiting until their breathing settled. "I've been telling myself I wasn't going to touch you, no matter how tempting. I didn't even last a week. You shatter my willpower to hell, and when I saw you in the hallway bleeding, some of my control snapped."

"I'm guilty, too. That was unprofessional, and despite how connected I feel to you, Jacob is your brother. I won't risk my relationship with him to explore the attraction between us."

"Guilty is the last thing I'm feeling." He dipped his finger under her chin, gently lifting her face. "I'm not going to play games. Straight up, Brynn, I want that to happen again, but more than that, I want to keep getting to know you, and that is completely separate from the care you give my brother. If things don't go the way I think they will, I swear I'll never keep you from Jacob if you want to break it off. You should know, though, I plan on doing everything in my power to keep you in my life, too."

She could only stare at him, mouth agape. Never had a man been so straightforward with her, but Neo wasn't the majority. No, he was something special. She tried to tamp down the glow surrounding her heart at his confession, but it was already blinding.

He circled her waist and lifted her off the countertop with ease. "Go relax for a bit. I'll fill up the tub."

"I'd like to help you," she said. Neo hadn't moved his hands from their place on her hips. She liked them there. Maybe a bit too much.

"You can help by sitting right where you were, giving the dog some moral support during his bath." He leaned down and kissed the tip of her nose. His sweet gestures continued to surprise her. She'd never known soft and tender growing up, at least not until Nana took her away.

"That sounds a lot like the help I gave you cooking dinner last night," she teased. "But I need to check on Jacob."

Neo released her and yanked the shower curtain to the side, the metal rings zinging across the rod. "He's just watching an episode of *South Park*."

She halted and gave him a sideways glance.

"Just kidding. That was a joke." He knelt down and switched on the taps. The dog turned his head from left to right as the pipes rattled and water gurgled out of the faucet. "He's watching *The Simpsons*."

Brynn rolled her eyes, a smile still on her face, and went to check on Jacob. Neo had positioned him on the couch, surrounded by pillows and a blanket. It was no wonder he'd decided to take a nap. She pulled the blankets up some more, placed a kiss on his head, and returned to the bathroom. Neo and the dog were sitting by the edge of the bathtub. He stroked the dog's head, murmuring soft endearments. Who knew this big, tough SEAL would baby-talk a dog?

"All right, buddy, in you go." He lifted the gentle giant with care and lowered him into the tub. The big mutt didn't seem to mind, lying down and stretching out as far as he could in the water. Dirt seeped off his fur and permeated the bath, turning it from clear to murky gray in seconds.

"I'd like to help." Brynn frowned at the dog's state. How long had the poor animal been on its own?

"He's pretty dirty, sweetheart." His hand skimmed along the top of the water, over the animal's protruding spine. "Don't want you getting an infection in those cuts on your hand. You could pass me some soap and get a clean towel ready." Brynn nodded, happy to contribute somehow, even if it was just to keep her busy. She slid off of the countertop and went to the closet. Fluffy towels were stacked in neat rows, and it didn't take long to find some liquid soap. When Neo reached up with his dry hand and took the bottle, their skin touched, spreading tingles and goose bumps up her arms. Still holding the towel, she slid back up on the countertop.

Neo lathered up the dog, his shirt now covered in dirty water. The dog's tail wound back and forth like a propeller, tongue lolling out the side of his mouth. As Neo scrubbed the fur along his belly and legs, his expression grew hard. His lips were pressed into a thin line, brow furrowed.

"Do you think someone is missing him?"

Neo pulled the drain plug. "Yeah, I'm sure they are, but no way in hell they're getting him back."

"Why, what's wrong?" She pushed off of the counter and crouched beside Neo.

"See." He pointed to the jagged gouges. "He's got bite marks all over his legs and stomach. Some completely healed over. Some that look to be a few weeks old." As the water drained lower and lower, her stomach began to churn.

"What do you think happened to him?" Unable to stop herself, she reached out and stroked the side of the dog's head. He leaned into her, starved for affection.

"He's a bait dog," Neo rumbled. Now that the tub was drained, he turned on the faucet again and used a cup to pour clean water over the dog, washing away any remaining dirt.

"What is that?" The injuries were horrific. It looked as though chunks of flesh had been torn from the bone.

"Some people breed and train dogs for underground fighting." He shook his head. "They test their dog's aggressiveness by putting them up against a dog that can't or won't fight back."

Heat prickled her eyes. "That's disgusting."

"Can't imagine someone hurting an animal." Neo draped the towel over the dog, gently rubbing his coat dry. "It's about as low as you can go."

"And yet he still sweet and good-natured." Her voice was thick with emotion. She hated to think about anything enduring pain.

"I know someone else like that, and she's pretty damn special. Strong as hell."

Her heart rate kicked up a notch at his words. Her mind was still raveled up about the kiss they shared. Intense and mind-blowing. A total out-of-body experience. If she felt that way from one kiss, what would it be like to make love to him?

A low groan broke from his lips. "Whatever you were just thinking, I want to know."

Her cheeks heated. In fact, she'd be surprised if she didn't have a full-body blush. "I was thinking about when you kissed me and how good it felt, and what…more would feel like."

He dragged in a ragged breath, holding her gaze for one moment, then two. After lifting the dog from the tub and giving him one more rubdown, he turned to her.

"I want to show you. Want you in my bed, my name on

your lips. I want to worship and taste every inch of you. But, while I'm looking forward to that a hell of a lot, I'd never rush you into anything. I want to know you, not just your body. I like spending time with you, any way I can get it."

Words were temporarily lost to her, so she nodded. Brynn couldn't deny that Neo's words gave her a thrill, but she was far from experienced, while he was a SEAL who'd probably had plenty of beautiful women. What would happen if they got together? She was already experiencing strong feelings for Neo. If they took things to the next level, she'd quickly grow more attached. Despite his assertion that he'd never get between her and Jacob, she was worried about how she would react if things ended. It would hurt like hell to see him every day, but she'd never abandon Jacob. The decision to test the waters with Neo was something she couldn't take lightly.

He cleared his throat. "I'm going to get this guy some food, then shower so I can wrap my arms around you without getting you soaked in grime." He leaned over and removed the towel from the floor, flinging it into the now-empty bath. She led the way to the kitchen with the dog prancing behind her like a show pony. The tub had done wonders for the animal's confidence. When she didn't hear footsteps behind her, she turned. Neo was standing a few feet from the kitchen, staring at the back of Jacob's wheelchair. He dipped his chin to his chest as he drew an expansive breath. "I was so caught up in everything that was going on, I missed this."

She took a few steps closer. Neo was tracing his finger over the sticker that read, *Proud Brother of a United States*

Sailor. "Jacob was happy when we found that."

"You know, I never considered myself a particularly lucky person." He studied the sticker as he spoke. "Most of the good things in my life have come from my own sweat and blood. Jacob, though? He's the exception." Neo glanced up at her. His eyes were glassy, flooded with emotion. "When he looks me in the eyes and smiles, something inside me brightens. I can't explain it, but having him here with me means the world."

"For him, too." Her own eyes stung at Neo's reaction to the simple lettering on vinyl. Neo straightened and closed the distance between them, pulling her into a hard hug. She rested her cheek on his chest, the rapid beat of his heart thumping against her face. Jacob and Neo were both incredibly lucky to have each other. That made her doubly blessed to have both of them in her life.

CHAPTER THIRTEEN

IN THE SHADOWS of an alley, Ronald Glen clenched his fists. His mark had disappeared inside an apartment complex, and what should've been an easy payday again dissolved to shit. He'd found her simple enough in the town outside Boston. The apartment's security was a joke, and he'd set himself up a nice little stakeout by the garbage residents had piled up blocking the back exit. Even the fire alarms were out of order, and the place was so filled with smoke he could discreetly light up a cigarette, and no one would be the wiser. She'd been alone, except for the kid in the wheelchair, and he wouldn't get in the way. He had planned to wait until nightfall, sneak upstairs, and shoot her where she slept.

Then that huge bastard had busted into the building. The guy was a mercenary if he'd ever seen one, leaving him to wonder who the hell the lady had pissed off enough to have two hits out on her. He was content to sit back and let the other guy do the dirty work and tell his client the job was done. He almost pissed himself when the man left with his mark and the kid. So shocked, he dropped his cigarette right into the trash heap. Tracking them had been a bitch, and he'd had to dip into his funds to get a hotel room so he could keep an eye on them.

The next day they'd hopped a flight to Virginia—another expense to hit his wallet. The client had paid extra for him to rough her up a bit before he killed her, but after all the trouble he'd been through, he'd forgo that part of the deal and pocket the cash. The guy who hired him would never know the difference. By the time he got released from Walpole, he'd be sitting on a beach in Mexico, enjoying a well-deserved retirement.

Only today hadn't gone as planned either. He should've shot that dirty mutt the second it started following him. Instead, he ignored it and stuck to the tree line, trying to get a shot off from a distance. The dog had run right into the road on the woman's heels, scaring her away. Now the dog was inside the apartment building with his mark, and he was standing in a piss-scented alley. Well, she better not get too comfortable because her number was up. The dog's, too.

CHAPTER FOURTEEN

NEO STOOD AT the kitchen sink, rinsing dishes from dinner the night before. The dog, who they'd collectively decided to call Oscar, sat dutifully at his feet, tail keeping time with the clank of the dishes that he methodically added to the washer. Three days had gone by since Neo had kissed Brynn on the bathroom countertop, and he could think of little else. He could still recall the way her body molded to his—a perfect fit.

A single touch of her lips had ignited something almost feral within him. She was his to protect and care for, just as Jacob was. Even a glimpse of the nicks and burns that were visible on her legs had made him murderous. He'd never allow anyone to harm her ever again. Sharing the same living space, with her laughter filling up his apartment, and her dimpled smile lighting him from the inside out was wonderful and torturous at the same time. With each passing minute he spent around her, the more he liked her. He was falling. Hard.

He'd always brushed off relationships as a waste of time. Always tried to convince others, and maybe himself, that family life wasn't something he wanted. Perhaps it was time to admit to himself that he wanted those things with a ferocity that extended to his soul. Still, he told himself time and time again not to depend on anyone but himself. The Teams had proved him wrong, but his own mother hadn't given a single care about him. He wasn't afraid he'd turn around and treat his own family that way—if he ever had one—but it wasn't like he had the best examples of stable relationships in his life.

Over the short span of a week and a half, Brynn had begun to unravel his mother's lies. She saw the best in people, and he wasn't an exception. Brynn was constantly building him up, making sure he acknowledged that there was another side of him that was warm and loving. With her constant encouragement, even he began to think of himself as more than the cold bastard his mother claimed he was.

Brynn was getting harder and harder to resist. Not even waiting to see if their offer on the home had been accepted kept his mind from wandering to the scent of honeyed lavender and the weight of endless midnight hair fisted in his hands. They'd worked together to complete Jacob's paperwork for the public middle school and get copies of his medical records. They were lucky that this school system was not only able to meet Jacob's needs but had several other students with similar disabilities, so the classroom already had a dedicated school nurse. His brother would start classes on Monday morning, but first, they were taking a tour and meeting his classmates.

"Almost ready," Brynn called from Jacob's bedroom. He'd insisted that she take his bed for now, and he was bunking on an air mattress in Jacob's room. That first night, they'd stayed up until one o'clock in the morning. He told Jacob stories about his own childhood and Hell Week during

BUD/S training. His brother had laughed, presumably at him, not with him—because there wasn't a damn thing funny about the training—when he had told him about the fragmented sleep, hours swimming in ice-cold water, and pushing his body past the limits of exhaustion. The kid's full-bellied laugh made his heart swell. Jacob had given him something he'd never thought possible—a chance to be a brother. To have a family outside the Teams. This was a mission he would not fail.

After they visited the school, he had a surprise for Brynn. Silver, Branch, and even Joker were coming over to the apartment to hang with Jacob. He was taking Brynn on a date.

He loaded the last dish in the washer, tossed a detergent pod in the dispenser, and hit the start button.

"Okay, we're ready." Brynn came into the room, hair loose around her shoulders, pushing Jacob. She paused by Oscar, leaning down to kiss him on the nose. The dog reveled in the attention, rolling onto his back in hopes of a belly rub. She let go of Jacob's chair to bend over and pet the dog's stomach. *Christ.* Her ass filling out a pair of jeans was a thing of fucking beauty. Brynn's giggle filled his chest with warmth, like someone had lit a match within him.

"Might want to avoid the kisses until the vet calls with the results of his lab work." His lips twitched with a suppressed smile. She brought that out in him—the light. Just knowing she and Jacob were here when he returned from base the past few days had given him a sense of anticipation. There was a reason to rush home for once.

She scrunched up her face. Adorable. "He can have all

the kisses he wants." She started to walk past him, but he hooked an arm around her waist in a playful hold and stepped up behind her.

"And me?" he whispered. Her hair was so soft against his cheek. He brushed it to the side, exposing the slope of her shoulders. He leaned down and planted a kiss at the nape of her neck. She shivered against him, her body instantly reacting to his touch.

"Not if we're going to make it to the school on time for our meeting." Her lips curved, and dimples popped in her cheeks. *Goddamn.* He liked that she was getting comfortable enough to tease him a bit.

Jacob let out an exasperated sigh.

"We're going," he said with a laugh. Jacob deserved an explanation of his relationship with Brynn. At the least about his growing feelings. One that they would have very soon.

Outside, a balmy breeze carried the scent of the ocean, and sunshine poured over the parking lot, reflecting metallic rays over the glossed paint of the vehicles. He planned to follow the same route Brynn had mentioned taking the day before. Maybe it was a long shot, but he wanted to see if anything looked out of the ordinary. He was still uneasy about the man Brynn thought she'd seen in the hotel, and then the scare she and Jacob had when they'd been out on a walk.

"Neo?" She paused on the pavement.

"Yeah?" He grinned, anticipating the next words.

"Where's the rental?" Her brows were drawn together and she was glancing around. This was the first time they'd ventured out together, and he'd told Brynn he'd rented an accessible van. Silver had already found him two accessible SUVs, though one wouldn't be delivered until the end of the month.

"I thought an upgrade was in order." He smiled over his shoulder as he walked toward the rear of a shiny black SUV. "And it's not a rental. Silver found it at a nearby dealership, and it's ours." There wasn't a car parked in the space to the left, so Neo pressed the key fob, opened the door, and hit the switch to lower the ramp to the side of the vehicle.

"Wow! It looks much simpler to operate than the old van." She skirted Jacob's chair and ruffled his hair. "What do you think?" The smile stretched across his face was pure elation.

She stepped closer, eyes widening when she noticed the bumper sticker on the back window. "Your brother has a new bumper sticker, too." Her voice had dropped an octave as she took another step closer to the sticker. "It says: *My brother, my hero.*"

BRYNN'S CHEST EXPANDED at the words printed over the symbol of a green ribbon, marking cerebral palsy awareness. Unshed tears burned behind her lids, and once again, she was so grateful that the brothers had found each other.

Jacob was still grinning when Neo walked up to his chair and cupped the back of his head. Neo dropped his forehead to Jacob's and whispered something she couldn't quite make out. She didn't need to hear the words though for a wedge to lodge painfully in her throat. What had been the reason for

Fergus's hate? For her parents' tremendous loyalty to their firstborn? She didn't often give in to self-pity, but the instant love Neo and Jacob shared made her envious for the relationship she'd never have, not only with her brother, but with her parents, too. They had made their decision to choose one child over the other, and had never tried to contact her since. The rejection was a wound that would never heal. Just when she thought it had scabbed over and she could move on, it ripped open again. The shock of the pain was enough to double her over. After they'd checked out all the new features in the car and secured Jacob's wheelchair, they pulled onto the main road headed toward the school.

As they drove, the light kept catching on the burnished dog tags hanging from the mirror. She reached up and brushed one of her fingers over the metal. "Are these Scooter's?" She swallowed heavily.

"Yeah. To remind me of his sacrifice. He gave his life so I could live mine. I won't take that for granted. No matter what situation I'm in, I will not give up. Even if I wished I were dead, I'd fight until my last breath, because anything else would tarnish Scooter's memory."

She ran a hand from his shoulder to his elbow, a lump sitting solidly in her throat as she internally whispered a thank-you to Neo's fallen teammate.

The rest of the drive to the school was silent, save for the pop songs Jacob loved blasting from the sound system. Neo slid his hand over the console and captured hers. The warmth of his skin and the strength of his grip were soothing. "Will you tell me about it?" His voice was low, and for the first time, she noticed his jaw was set like stone. When it came to her emotions, Neo was able to read her with precise accuracy. Pinning down her feelings should be impossible after nearly two weeks of knowing him. The poppies inked on his arm slipped into her head. Her grandmother did always adore a fanciful tale. How she would love knowing that a symbol of her was permanently etched on the man Brynn was losing her heart to.

"Brynn?" Neo's eyes were narrowed, searching her face.

"Sorry. Yes. I was just feeling a bit…lost."

"Your family let you down in the worst way possible, but Brynn? Don't think for a second you don't have people who love and care about you. You're part of our family now. This is your home." He squeezed her hand and hung on tight.

She hadn't even noticed that they'd pulled onto the school's long drive. Her eyes blurred, a convex lens of tears building and rippling over her lower lids. Of course Neo didn't mean *he* loved her. Cared about her, maybe, but his words still made her pulse jet.

Neo cut the wheel to the left and drove into an open space in the parking lot. The school was a sprawling construction of brick and glass. Butterflies bumped and banged around in her stomach. If she was anxious to see Jacob's new school, how did he feel?

"Here we are. Ready to go meet your teacher?" She lowered the rearview mirror to look at him behind her.

Jacob was unusually quiet, his eyes trained on the window.

"Are you nervous, bud?" Neo turned around in this seat, and put a hand on Jacob's knee. When he continued to stare out the window, Neo's pained gaze cut to Brynn. "I don't want him to be stressed out." He raked a jerky hand through his hair.

"He'll be okay. Jacob just likes to take it all in. Once he's comfortable he'll start responding again." After unlocking the four-point tie-down system on Jacob's wheelchair, they crossed the parking lot, and checked in at the office. Neo's body was rigid as he scanned the lobby with an intense expression. Every so often, he turned his gaze to Jacob.

"I've never seen him this withdrawn before." He stiffened, like he might jump up and wheel Jacob out of the school.

She put a hand on Neo's arm. "He's okay. Really."

Her touch seemed to calm him into sitting for a few more minutes. The scuff of shoes against tile had her shoulders sagging in relief. She didn't know how much longer she could keep Neo in the building. A middle-aged man in a yellow sweater vest and round-rimmed glasses approached them.

"Hello, folks. I'm Mr. Bloom." Brynn stood and took the hand he offered. His handshake was firm and his smile warm.

"Nice to meet you. I'm Jacob's nurse, Brynn."

"Neo Godfrey. Jacob's brother." Neo stepped closer to Jacob and put a protective hand on his shoulder.

Good grief. The way Neo's stare was boring into the teacher, he'd probably know every speeding ticket the poor man had received, if he paid his taxes, and how often he flossed his teeth by dinnertime.

"Jacob, welcome to Virginia Beach Middle School. I know it's probably a lot to take in, but we're so excited to have you here. Why don't we go meet the rest of the class?" Mr. Bloom turned his attention to her and Neo. "Right this way. We have some students very eager to meet you and—"

A shriek pierced the air, and a tall, lanky boy with reddish hair flew through the halls, a mischievous grin playing across his lips. A young woman chased after him, an iPad and clipboard in her hands. The boy cast a look over his shoulder every few steps to see if he was being followed, losing his coordination once or twice only to be saved by the narrow purple lockers lining the hall.

"Jacob, meet Collin. Collin, this is our new student—"

"Jacob Godfrey," Collin sang out, holding the note as long as his lungs allowed. "Hello, Jacob Godfrey." His hands were in constant motion, shaking back and forth like he was trying to dispel water droplets from his fingers. Collin didn't seem to mind that Jacob wasn't responding. "Mr. Bloom, Jacob Godfrey dressed as a peanut butter and jelly sandwich. You're butter, sunshine, corn, banana. Jacob Godfrey is peanut butter and jelly."

Brynn smiled. It was hard not to with Collin's enthusiasm. "I see what you mean," she said. "Jacob has a red shirt like strawberry jelly and brown pants like peanut butter."

Collin clapped and spun in a circle. The woman who had been on the boy's heels in the hallway caught up and explained she was the one of the teaching assistants in the class. They all started walking toward the classroom. Collin stayed by Jacob's side, pointing out all the colors of the school as they moved. Just as Neo had relaxed a fraction with the help of Collin's excited banter, Jacob's smile returned, and soon he was making shrieks back and forth with his new friend. Her chest expanded. This was a good place. A happy place.

They stopped at a classroom with a large textured sign on the door. Collin touched it before they entered. The moment they stepped inside, any fears she might've had about the transition eased. The room radiated warmth. There were giant beanbag chairs clustered in the corners and adaptive seating throughout the room. A large cylinder-shaped fish tank bubbled on a table.

"All right, class, this is Jacob, a new member of our crew." There were two additional staff members in the room, who both waved and greeted Jacob. Another child sitting in a wheelchair tilted her head toward an orange device. When her temple hit it, the tablet on her desk said, "Hello, nice to meet you."

Mr. Bloom introduced Jacob to the students. The noise and commotion were pulling Jacob back to the present. He blinked his eyes a few times, cocked his head back, and responded with a vocalization of his own. Neo visibly relaxed beside her.

"What's Jacob's day going to look like when he's in school?" she asked. Collin was still at Jacob's side, explaining everything in the room through color.

"We are going to do an evaluation to determine the best way to support Jacob. This will be his homeroom, but we'd like him to attend some inclusion classes around the school. He'll have a dedicated nurse and teaching assistant at all times."

Brynn continue to ask questions, and they talked about providing Jacob with something called a biosensor as another tool to communicate. By the time they left her mind was whirring with excitement over all the possibilities for Jacob. She slid into the passenger seat of the vehicle, the scent of leather and new car permeating the air of the interior.

Neo got behind the wheel and checked his phone. His expression turned serious. "We got an email from the Realtor."

She sucked in a breath and held it as Neo scanned the message he'd received. A smile flourished over his face, making his cheekbones more pronounced. In one fluid movement he was out of the SUV, opening the door to the back, and wrapping Jacob in a bear hug. "We got the house."

She clasped her hands to her chest and grinned. The home had everything Jacob would need to thrive, even in adulthood. Neo slid back into the front and tagged her around the back of the neck, pulling her forehead to his. There was a fluttering in her chest as he held her there. The small gesture made her feel special. Her fingers ached to curl into the material of his shirt to get even closer, but she was acutely aware of Jacob's presence.

Moving to Virginia with a man she'd just met had been one of the boldest decisions she'd ever made, but since the airplane touched down, something had settled inside her. She wasn't sure if it was peace or a sense of rightness, but she wanted to wrap up the feeling and hold it close. She knew better than most that things could change in an instant, and she wanted to hold on to the happy with all her might.

CHAPTER FIFTEEN

Neo's elation crashed to the ground the moment they stepped inside the apartment. Silver Branch, and Joker stood around the kitchen island, a trio of grim expressions on their faces. There was a charge in the air like the crackle and snap of adrenaline before they stepped into battle. He was pushing Jacob, and stopped abruptly. Brynn crashed into his back with a squeak. Oscar left the men he'd been sitting with and trotted over to them, his whole body shaking with excitement. The dog started with Jacob, lapping his tongue over his brother's hands, and then moved to him. The weight of the animal's paws hit his stomach as he attempted to stand on his hind legs to plant a slobbering wet kiss on his face.

"Let's save the kisses for Brynn and Jacob." He ran his hand down the dog's back, which seemed less bony already. Oscar saved his most exuberant dance for Brynn, desperately trying to lick her face and nudge her.

"Seems like the new addition is working out." Silver was leaning over the counter, his elbows resting on the stone. The dog shuffled to his teammate's side, and he scratched Oscar behind the ear.

"He's a love." Brynn crouched down, and the dog took her movement as an open invitation to snuggle. He loved how her gorgeous eyes brightened and glowed with warmth when she encountered someone or something she cared about. She'd had an instant soft spot for the mutt, which had earned the dog a place in their home indefinitely.

"I heard congratulations are in order." Joker shifted and crossed his arms over his chest.

"Yeah, I'm pumped. Finally, we've got a friend with a pool." Branch moved around the counter and knelt beside Jacob's chair. "Heard you got yourself one hell of a house. Congrats, man. You're going to invite us over, right?"

Instead of responding, Jacob just chuckled.

"He's going to charge you to use the pool, Branch."

Despite their easy banter, there was a strain weighing down on his teammates. They needed to talk to him alone. His suspicions were confirmed when all eyes fell to him, silently communicating that they needed to talk. Shit. He had wanted Brynn and Jacob settled into the new house before they left on a mission. Or maybe they'd discovered new information on Fergus. He hadn't told Brynn that he'd asked the guys to check on Fergus's location and his activity in the past ten years. He didn't want to upset her, but regardless, keeping her safe was more important.

As though she sensed his team's urgency, she cleared her throat. "Jacob and I are going to play a game."

When they were out of earshot, he turned to his brothers. "Give it to me," he demanded.

"You're not going to like this. One of the tech guys called me this morning. Fergus is no longer in Ireland." Silver scrubbed his hands over his face.

"Where the fuck is he, then?" His stomach rolled.

"That's the bad part." Branch's expression was grim. Tension wrapped around his body, stiffening his muscles and making his jaw ache. He didn't need his team to tell him what he already knew in his gut. A man like Fergus, with a tendency to kill things he perceived to be weaker than himself, was not going to forget his little sister.

"He's here in the United States. The same place he's been for the past six years."

Neo slammed his fist down on the counter. "Fuck. Where is he?"

"Well, if there's any good in this, it's that he's been incarcerated for five of those years in Walpole. It's a maximum state prison in Massachusetts."

He flexed his fingers and curled his hands into fists. "All this time, he's been in the same state as Brynn."

"Yeah. Don't tell me that's a coincidence." Joker pushed away from the counter and began to pace.

"What did he do?" Neo stalked to the refrigerator and tugged it open, reaching down for a bottle of water. Condensation trickled across his palm, coating his fingers.

"Attacked a woman, threw her in his car, then tossed her from the moving vehicle. She survived her injuries, but he did a number on her. The court tried to go for murder one, but the jury deliberated, and ultimately he was only charged with aggravated assault." Silver's frown deepened.

"That's bullshit." This situation was going to rock Brynn to the core. Her sense of safety was going to be blown to hell. "The things he did—"

"He's not gonna lay a hand on her, Neo." Joker rounded the island and gripped his shoulder. "She's yours and Jacob's and that makes her ours, too." Joker might've been suspicious of Brynn at first, but her kindness was undeniable. He'd thawed to her bit by bit, and now when Joker looked at her, there was a thread of envy in his eyes.

"Look at this picture." Silver's face was set. Hard lines and a frown added to his severe expression.

Silver slid his iPad to the edge of the table. *Abducted Woman Thrown from Moving Car.* The air around him thinned and spots flooded his vision. A picture of the victim was published with the article. Straight black hair, pale skin, and bright blue eyes stared back at him.

"Do you think he thought that was Brynn or do you think he was planning to use this woman as a warm-up before going after her? Christ, the victim could pass as Brynn's sister," Branch said.

Something clattered to the ground behind them. Brynn was standing just beyond the kitchen. The color had leached from her face, and her eyes were wide and full of terror.

"Who could've been my sister?" Her voice trembled. "And what happened to her?" She kept her hand plastered to the wall for support. "Is Fergus here? In the United States?"

He crossed the room and took her into his arms. Her body was trembling all over. The damage her brother had done was unforgivable. He scooped Brynn up, cradling her, and lowered himself down on one of the kitchen chairs. She buried her face against his chest, a move that caused a fierce blaze of protectiveness to blast through him. Maybe it was an archaic way of thinking, but since the moment he saw Brynn, something had clicked. They were two parts of a whole and he'd do whatever it took to protect her.

"We all have your back. That shithead would have to come through four Navy SEALs to get to you and Jacob. Not fucking likely." Silver went to the fridge, dug out another bottle of water from the back, and brought it over to her.

"Thanks." He dipped his chin and removed one hand from Brynn's hip to take the bottle. "Take a few sips of this, sweetheart. Everything is going to be okay." Better damn be, or Fergus would be begging him to bury his KA-BAR knife into his chest.

"I've brought this to your doorstep. By just being here, I could be putting Jacob and the four of you at risk. If I pack up and disappear, Fergus will have no reason to come here."

His arms banded around her, a low growl vibrating from his throat.

Branch came over and dropped to one knee. "Honey, we are all well-honed government weapons. We're not afraid of a sorry excuse for a human who preys on animals and women. If he comes after you, we'll gladly disperse him to hell."

"I'm tired of being afraid. Wasn't it enough that our parents believed him? Chose him? He never should've come here."

"He never should've gotten away with what he did." He stroked Brynn's polished hair, loving how she leaned into his touch.

"I need to know what happened." She tilted her chin, angling her face up to him. She may look delicate, but this woman was anything but. Some of the fear that clouded her irises had hardened to determination. He wouldn't insult her by withholding the truth.

"I asked the team to look into your brother's whereabouts. They came back with some new information. Your brother traveled to the United States six years ago. After a year, he was arrested for taking a woman against her will, and throwing her from a moving vehicle; she got lucky."

Brynn swung her legs to the floor and jumped up, pacing over to the island. The tablet was within reach and she grabbed it. The screen brightened and Brynn drew in a sharp breath. "She does look like me. Was hurt because of me."

"No." He winced at the sharpness in his voice and stood, nearly knocking the chair to the floor. "The only one responsible for that woman's injuries is Fergus. Do not blame yourself."

"Where is he now?" Brynn took a few steps toward him and he pulled her into a hug.

"Federal state prison. He won't be going anywhere anytime soon, but we wanted you to know so you can be prepared and on alert."

A bitter laugh broke from her lips. "I've been on alert for what feels like most of my life."

"The difference is you're not alone now. We've got your back, Brynn. If he came for you, things would end poorly for him. Plus, it would be difficult to escape Walpole." Silver crossed his arms firmly over his chest.

"I thought you came here to meet Oscar." She swiped her fingers beneath her eyes, brushing away tears.

"They actually came over here because I asked them to hang out with Jacob. I want to take you to dinner if you think you're up for it."

Brynn looked far too pale. "I—I think I'd rather stay in, but thank you for the nice offer." She turned and left the room.

"Has to be a hell of a big shock." Branch was on his feet, raking both hands through his hair. "Go make sure she's all right. We'll hang out with Jacob like we planned. Order some pizzas or something."

"'Preciate it." The men in front of him were his family. If something happened to him on a mission or otherwise, they'd care for Jacob and Brynn. His chest expanded with love for his brothers. They could be a pain in the ass, each stubborn and set in his own ways, but when shit hit the fan, there wasn't anyone he'd rather have at his back. He found Jacob listening to an audiobook in the living room and explained that the guys had come over to spend time with him, then went in search of Brynn. Fergus might be locked away, but the fine hairs on the back of his neck were standing upright, and dread soured in his stomach.

CHAPTER SIXTEEN

BRYNN BURIED HER face into Oscar's fur. He'd followed her into the bedroom and stretched out beside her. His head was resting on the same pillow, and every so often, he stretched his paw out to her, offering comfort. She needed time to regroup. Time to think about how to handle the knowledge that Fergus had been so close for years. He had lived in the same state for six years. How was that possible? Her stomach churned and bile burned up her throat. An innocent woman had received a punishment meant for her. Had Fergus stumbled on the woman by chance and grabbed her, thinking it was his sister? Or had he simply abducted her because of their likeness? Her gut told her that it was the first. Fergus must've been shocked and enraged when he saw that the woman wasn't her after all and had impulsively thrown her from the vehicle. If he took her for the latter reason, the woman wouldn't have lived. Fergus would've wanted to play his sick games with her.

There was a tap on the door before it creaked open. She had the curtains drawn, but light spilled in from the hallway. She nearly turned to face the person who had entered, but she forced herself to remain still. Her mind knew that is was Neo, but anxiety pumped into her chest, demanding she look for herself that there was no danger present.

Oscar's tail beat against the bed, and his tongue lolled out of his mouth. Neo's footsteps padded across the room. Then came the sound of him unlacing his shoes, and each one falling to the floor at the side of the bed.

The mattress dipped with his weight as he lifted the covers and climbed in beside her. He put his arm around her waist and drew her close. Oscar's body was sprawled along her front and Neo was at her back. The body heat from both of them was beginning to warm the chill that had settled down to her bones. His heart steadily pounded into her back, and his chest expanded as he drew in a long, satisfied breath. She loved how he seemed to always be inhaling her. Like he was coating his lungs in her scent and couldn't get enough. Sure, her life had been crazy the past week, but she'd never felt safer or more cared for. There was so much to be grateful for between Jacob, Neo, and his team. Even Joker had tried to reassure her in the kitchen.

"Tell me what you're thinking, sweetheart." His breath was hot on her neck, filling her belly with warmth.

"There was so much desperation, so much loneliness as a kid. What if knowing that Fergus is here makes me stumble back into the anxiety and paranoia of my childhood?"

"I'm not going to tell you there won't be times when you feel that way. After coming back from the mission that killed Scooter, I heard his final scream and the explosion ringing in my ears for weeks. There are times when I still wake up in a cold sweat. Other times when I have to abandon my cart at the grocery store and walk out because the churning of the ice machine or the beep of a cash register triggers something. I need to get out so I can breathe. After, well, I can't deny that it doesn't make me feel vulnerable." He ran his hand up and down the length of her exposed arm.

"I want to be strong and capable. That's what you and Jacob both deserve." Sometimes she didn't feel that way, though. "When you go on a mission, the last thing I want you doing is worrying that I can't handle things here. That Jacob's not being cared for as he should."

"I will be thinking about you, but it won't be because I think you're not capable of caring for my brother." His left hand was pinned beneath her waist and the mattress, and he lowered it a fraction, gripping her hip with possessive fingers. A thrill skated through her. "Your laugh, the way your dimples indent your cheeks, how your body fits so fucking perfect against mine. That's what I'll be thinking of. What won't cross my mind for a second is you being incapable of doing something."

"When Nana and I arrived in the United States, healing was a slow process, but having her with me, someone I could depend on, helped immensely. I found the more I helped others, the better I felt inside. I turned into someone I could like and respect. Someone dependable and smart. Someone who could be called upon in an emergency situation and take control." She released a long breath. "Now, though, it feels like that progress has taken a hit. I haven't been able to control my shaking since you mentioned his name. I should be past that. I should be fuming, not scared to death that he might escape or send someone after me." She was so close to having everything she ever wanted. Why couldn't the past just stay where it was meant to?

"I'm so sorry, sweetheart." He nuzzled into her hair, his

fingers caressing her arms up and down, offering comfort, offering his strength. "If our roles were reversed, I can't imagine how I would feel knowing he was here. The guys are looking up the extent of his sentence. He won't be available to appeal for parole for some time, but if and when that does happen, and he's out of the confines of the prison, we will take care of him." His hands tightened on her. "He'll never get near you. He signed his own death sentence the day he got on a plane to America." He was rubbing circles on her back, hands dipping over her hip.

"I couldn't live with myself if you or any of your teammates got sent to prison for killing him. I have to believe that the law will take care of things. I wonder if my parents knew he was coming here. I hope not, because no matter how much they hate me, it would kill me if they didn't contact me. To at least warn me that Fergus was coming to America. Maybe they could lie to themselves and say the abuse never happened, but the scars were there in plain sight."

"They didn't deserve you then, Brynn, and they sure as hell don't deserve you now. From here on out, they don't exist for you. Nothing you did or didn't do as a child turned them into the cold, selfish people who would let their daughter be abused." She could feel Neo tense behind her. A sudden chill cased his words.

"I don't want to put you or Jacob at risk."

"Don't talk like that. You're staying. This is your home. I want you in my life, not just Jacob's. I know it's fast, but it's right. If I had to fight through an army to keep you, I'd do it in a heartbeat." His breath mingled over the sensitive skin of her neck, sending tingles down her spine.

"I'm afraid to believe what I'm feeling for you. Afraid that you'll wake up and realize what you thought you felt was just gratitude for taking care of Jacob."

"I am grateful, Brynn, but if that's all I felt, I wouldn't have the urge to slip into your bed at night simply to hold you. I wouldn't long to hear your voice when I'm on base training, even if it's only for a few hours. I wouldn't be thinking of a future together, because even after a short two weeks the thought of being apart from you physically hurts." He smoothed his palm down her hair. "Now that the offer on the house is accepted, the guys will help us move our stuff in. There's a local security company in the area with a great reputation. I'm going to see if they can come out to the property tomorrow and fast-track a new security system, because chances are we're going to be called out within the next month and I want you to feel secure when I'm not here. No one will be able to sneak up on the house without you knowing about it, or having an instant connection to law enforcement."

"That sounds like it's going to cost a fortune. And what you're already paying for the house…I feel like I'm taking advantage. I already told you the amount you deposited into my account for the months your mother stopped paying my salary was unnecessary and excessive."

"I'm not trying to sound arrogant, but there is no shortage of money. I've lived simply and invested well. Making sure you and Jacob have everything you want and need gives me peace. Making sure you're both safe and comfortable is exactly what I want to spent my money on. I don't want you feeling like you owe me anything. The security is for all of us, as is the home. Fergus will never get his hands on you."

"Sometimes I feel so weak. The moment I heard his name, I started trembling. I don't want to be some cowering frightened victim that you feel the need to protect. I don't know how to be brave now that I know he's so close."

"You're braver than you think. You survived years of abuse. Years of others not believing your story. I can't imagine how crushing that must've been. The toll it took on your psyche. And yet you're kind and passionate about what you do. When your grandmother passed away, even when you were alone here, you did what needed to be done. When my mother left you high and dry, you did what was necessary to get a roof over Jacob's head. There's nothing weak about you."

Neo's hands began wandering over her stomach, and the touch went from comforting to sensual. The dog took the hint and wandered to the end of the bed and jumped off onto the floor. With every breath she took, her erect nipples strained against the thin material of her bra. Neo shifted, propping himself up on one elbow. He kissed a trail, gentle and sweet, down to the curve of her neck. His tongue swirled against her skin, making everything pulse and ache.

"Mmm." She couldn't stop the sigh that escaped her lips. Neo's hand skimmed up her stomach and over her rib cage, pausing right below the swell of her chest.

"Is this okay? Can I touch you?"

"Please." She arched her back, and his hands cupped her, massaging in slow, deliberate circles, touching everywhere but the sensitive tips. She arched into him again, this time her bottom nudging against his swollen erection. He groaned and a flood of heat seared through her, gathering at the apex of her thighs. Finally, he rolled the hard nubs between his fingers. Electricity shot through her and traveled straight to the soles of her feet. Nothing had ever felt better. She rolled, turning into him.

"That's it, sweetheart. Come here." His strong arms banded around her for one heartbeat, then two, before he went back to stroking her. He worked her shirt up, and lowered his head, sucking one nipple into his mouth through the mesh of her bra before turning his attention on the other. Her panties were damp and a visceral ache, an emptiness that she'd never felt before, pulsed at her core. His fresh scent tickled her nostrils as the combined sensation of his tongue, the scrape of his teeth, and the now-damp material of her bra created a delicious friction. He lifted his head, and she nearly groaned in protest, the cool air of the bedroom replacing the heat of his mouth. He pressed a kiss to her forehead, then her eyelids and cheeks. The sweet gesture swelled in her throat, making any words near impossible.

Angling her chin, she met his lips. This was the first kiss they'd shared since their explosive encounter on the bathroom countertop. In the few days since, they shared brief touches and the occasional brush of lips. The need for more had been building within her, and now with each stroke of his tongue, she felt as though she were catching fire, burning from the inside out.

She dipped her fingers beneath his shirt, outlining the hard lines of muscle, rubbing her thumbs over his nipples.

His groan vibrated along her lips and quickened the pace of their kiss, pushing deeper against her. She hooked her fingers at the waistline of his jeans, slipping her fingers between fabric. His skin was feverish, and the head of his erection brushed her fingers, already leaking from the tip. His hands jerked, catching her wrists. His chest heaved, breath rushing in and out.

"Fuck. I didn't mean for that to get out of hand. I don't want to take advantage of the situation, Brynn."

"I'm not kissing you because I'm scared. I'm kissing you because ever since that first time, I can't forget how you taste. The way my body catches fire when you're close. I've never had that before. Nothing's ever felt this good."

Neo groaned, the sound bordering on pain. "Haven't even made you come yet, sweetheart."

She licked her lips, and laid her cheek against his chest while her breathing slowed. "I wouldn't know. I don't think I, ah, ever have." Heat scored her cheeks. Why had she admitted that out loud?

"Christ, sweetheart. When I take you there, you'll know. There will be no mistaking it."

There was a light knock on the door. "Guys, we're taking Jacob to the park across the street. Back in an hour."

"Be careful," Neo barked back. When the front door to the apartment slammed shut, he sighed and buried his face in the crook of her neck before pulling back and studying her face.

"Brynn, make no mistake, I want you, but when I'm moving inside you, there will be no fear surrounding us. It will just be you and me." He lowered his head, kissing her in slow, soft strokes. His taste was intoxicating. The feel of his hard body beneath her hands, grounding. He shifted, bracing himself above her. "I'm a selfish bastard, though." His teeth playfully dragged at her bottom lip. "And you're not leaving this bed until I have the taste of your first orgasm on my tongue."

Her body reacted instantly to his crass words, and a flush of warmth settled between her hips. She tilted her head back, exposing her neck. He nibbled at the delicate skin of her collarbone.

"Arms up," he demanded and she immediately submitted. There was something sensual and exciting about following his command. Down to her soul, she knew he would never intentionally hurt her. That he only sought to give her pleasure and happiness. He peeled the shirt up and over her head, then reached behind her back and unclasped her bra, tossing it to the floor. He immediately lowered his mouth, flicking his tongue against one stiff peak, sucking and nipping, before shifting to the other side. She was writhing against him. Her panties were soaked as he continued to move lower. That had never happened before, and she wasn't sure if she should be embarrassed or if it was normal.

He grazed and licked a trail down her rib cage and stomach, still plumping and caressing her breasts as he continued his exploration. She was panting, her groin throbbing in painful waves.

"I get it now. Everything feels so good, but it's too much."

She felt his lips curve against her skin, and he looked up, desire burning in his eyes. "I haven't even gotten started yet."

He pushed off of the bed and, hooking his hands behind her knees, pulled her closer to the edge. The rough pads of his fingers skimmed along her waist as he positioned them at the top of her jeans and tugged, removing the material, underwear and all, in one fluid motion. She closed her legs, suddenly feeling too exposed.

His gaze raked over her body before he kneeled on the floor at the end of the bed. "You're gorgeous." He caressed her hips reverently. "Fucking perfection." His voice was low and gruff, making her heart pound even harder. "Open your legs, sweetheart."

She dropped her knees to the side, feeling more than a little self-conscious at the intimate position. With a wicked grin he lowered his head and nipped her inner thigh, soothing the light sting with his tongue. His ragged breaths caressed her exposed skin, and when he dragged his tongue up her center, she fisted her hands in the sheets. Her mind went blank as he circled his tongue around her opening, and all she could do was feel. A shudder swept through her as his tongue teased her inner folds. The sensations were too much and not enough at the same time. She let go of the sheets and raked her fingers over his short hair. A groan broke from his lips, vibrating straight through her.

She continued to massage his scalp as he licked the flat of his tongue up to her clit. Her hands fell back to the sheets, trying to find something to hang on to as he lapped and stroked at the sensitive bundle of nerves. When he pressed one finger inside her, she bore down, welcoming the pressure. Her breath was coming in shallow pants. She squirmed against his tongue and fingers. Maybe she'd be embarrassed by her actions later, but right now, her thighs were quaking as she rocked her hips against him. When a second finger stretched inside her and he sucked her most sensitive spot, pleasure exploded within her until she was shuddering and slicked with sweat. Aftershocks seized her body, and he gentled his touch, bringing her down slowly.

She lay on the bed, temporarily stunned, trying to drag oxygen into her lungs. Neo had been right. If she'd had an orgasm before, she certainly would've known. She was still trapped in a haze of sensation when the mattress dipped and he settled beside her. He didn't pressure her for words or conversation, instead caressing slow circles over her skin.

Neo had given her so many firsts. He was the first man to hold her while she slept, the first to ignite her body with one kiss. The one who brought her insurmountable pleasure. He was also the first man she'd lost her heart to. He was right that these feelings were too soon, but there they were nonetheless. All the people who'd let her down groused in the back of her mind, but she brushed the thought away. Neo was different. After her nana had died, she was convinced there wasn't anyone she could rely on but herself. The honorable SEAL at her side proved her theory wrong every single day. It was up to her to take the chance and see what would happen if she placed her faith in him.

CHAPTER SEVENTEEN

NEO LAY BESIDE Brynn, listening to her breathing as it evened out. Her taste was still on his tongue, the feel of her fingers digging into his scalp branded into his mind. Every little sound and whimper she made was committed to memory. The way she'd exploded beneath his touch had given him a profound sense of satisfaction. He would forever treasure being the first man to bring her to the edge, to give her such mindless pleasure that she gripped his headboard and bowed against him. She set off something primal within him, and he wanted to claim her as his own. Little did she know that she already held his heart and body. No one but her would ever do. She was it for him. Another woman would never set foot in his home, certainly not his bed. The mere thought of it was abhorrent. He'd never loved a woman before and he'd never love another again.

"Brynn." He propped himself up on his elbow. Her hair was mussed, the black strands tangled over his white sheets. Her skin was still flushed, and for a moment, he thought she'd fallen asleep. Then she opened one eye and peeked at him, before quickly closing it again. "What are you doing?" He chuckled.

She opened her eyes and rolled to her side, facing him, but she stared at his chest and cleared his throat.

"Was...ah...was that okay?"

His heart expanded, swamped with love. His girl hadn't been shy with his hands and mouth on her, but now she was avoiding his stare and had a healthy blush blooming over her cheeks. He gently lifted her chin. "Don't hide from me. What you gave me was a gift. I should be asking if you're okay." He rubbed his thumb over her jawline.

"That was so much more than I thought it would be. I don't think there's a word that describes how you made me feel. But what about you?" Her eyes moved down his body, stopping at the swell in his jeans.

"There'll be other times for that." Getting Brynn off had been incredible in itself, and he meant what he said. He planned to have a lot more time with her. *Forever.* "This was about you. Learning what you like."

"I liked everything." A shy smile quirked her lips.

"Glad to hear it." He stroked the tips of her hair. So damn soft. "I did, too. Don't think I'm ever going to get enough of you." He breathed her in. There would be a time soon that he'd have to go weeks, maybe even months without honey and lavender filling his nostrils. Knowing she was waiting for him, though? That would carry him through. "But if there's a time when you don't like something I do, inside or outside the bedroom, I need you to tell me. It would gut me if you were upset or went along with something you didn't want because you thought it would please me."

"That goes both ways, you know." Her grin broadened. A flash of radiance that tore the oxygen from his lungs.

"Deal," he said after a moment. "I promise not to hide

anything from you. That is, things that don't have to do with my job. There will be stuff I can tell you about where I'm going and what I'm doing, but for the most part I won't be able to share. I'm bound to silence in some areas. Is that going to be a problem?"

"I understand why and it's okay. Just don't keep things you can tell me, things that bother you bottled up, okay? I don't want to hand you over all my baggage if you're not going to let me unpack yours now and again." She kissed the tip of his nose, a tender gesture that unlocked a surge of peace within him.

He smiled at her, loving every single thing about this moment. "Okay, then. I'll let you sort my shit, too."

"The guys will be back with Jacob soon, won't they?" She stretched her hands over her head, arching her back so her bare breasts pressed into the material of his T-shirt. His cock flexed, but he ignored it, opting to tickle her right below the ribs instead. She shrieked and dissolved into laughter. His heart stretched, so fucking full, he imagined light seeping through the cracks of the underused organ.

"Probably soon." He rolled, taking her with him so she was positioned on top of his chest.

"I should get dressed." Her hair curtained around him, the connection between them deepening when she touched the side of his face with tender hands and soft, dazed eyes.

He leaned up and kissed her on the forehead. "I would vehemently reject that idea in nearly any other scenario." He planted two quick kisses on her lips and gave her bottom a teasing tap. "Up you go." He sat with her in his arms then placed her on the bed and went in search of her things.

"No sense in being uncomfortable." He retrieved yoga pants, a pair of panties, and a shirt. "I watched when you unpacked." He grinned at her in the mirror, laughing at the way her brow rose in question at his perusal of her things. He'd never been playful with anyone before. Not until Brynn. The back and forth teasing and light-heartedness was new for him. He constantly had the urge to wrap his arms around her and make her laugh—even if that resulted in a tickle attack. The guys would get a kick out of hearing that, but he didn't give the first fuck. If his teammates knew what it felt like to have their whole world shift, for their heart to catch fire with the most beautiful burn, they'd be envious.

A half hour later, they crowded around the living room after finishing the pizza the guys had brought home. Oscar lay on the rug, occasionally army crawling up to one of them looking for discarded pieces of crust. He'd already eaten enough pizza to fill a grown man. An oversized beanbag chair that hadn't been in the apartment before was cushioning Jacob like a nest. They were spoiling Jacob rotten any chance they got, including the colossal chair that they had seen in a shop on the way to the park. Silver and Joker flanked him, sitting on either side of the beanbag. Branch sat adjacent from the couch where he and Brynn were settled. He kept his arm around her, wanting to feel her close. There would be no mistaking his intentions toward her, but since the day his team picked them up at the airport, they'd known she was important.

"The VR headset was a great idea." Brynn's eyes softened as she watched Jacob's head turning from left to right, the virtual reality goggles strapped to his head. He had the same wide smile that he got when they went running. Just soaking in the experience. Despite Jacob's significant obstacles, he embraced life and savored everyday activities that others might take for granted. The bumper sticker he bought was no lie. His brother was his hero. To go through so much and still radiate light and joy was no small feat. He made those around him better by sharing that enthusiasm and quick acceptance. Jacob and Brynn were everything good in this world. Everything he fought to protect.

Joker shrugged, brushing off the compliment, but he sat a little straighter. "It's nothing. Sometimes I don't like to leave my place after a mission. These help me explore without setting foot outside."

"What's he watching?" Brynn asked, sinking into his side. God, he loved having her close. Loved when she sought out his touch.

"It's appropriate, Mom." Silver chuckled and shot Brynn a wink. He liked how his team had drawn Brynn into the fold. Even Joker had relaxed around her.

"A tour of Grand Teton National Park. Seems like he's loving it," Joker said.

"We'll go there for real someday." There was a vibration against Neo's hip, and he reached into his pocket and pulled out his phone. Oscar was on alert, sitting up with his head tilted to the side. Neo glanced at the screen, and suddenly his limbs hardened and grew heavy. "It's the commander." His voice was flat and empty. The usual adrenaline rush of an upcoming mission was absent.

"Lieutenant Commander Richardson, sir."

"Ransom, wheels up at oh seven hundred hours. We

have a confirmed location and we're ready to move."

"Yes, sir."

"Get some rest. The stakes are high. There is no room for error on this mission."

They disconnected, and he slid his phone onto the coffee table. He wasn't in a position where he could leave, but he didn't have a choice.

"That was the call," he told the team.

Joker slid the VR headset off of Jacob. "Wheels up, man. Mission time. I'm sorry we have to leave so soon. It's been fun getting to know you, kid. I'm gonna give this headset to Brynn, so you can keep it safe for me while I'm gone." Joker squeezed his brother's shoulder, and a pang settled in his heart.

There were so many things Neo had wanted to see through before he got called out on his next mission. Wanted to be moved into the new house, have the security system installed there, take Jacob to do some back-to-school shopping, and drive him to his first day of school. Brynn's new van would be available at the dealership in a week or so, and he'd wanted to surprise her. If they had discovered Fergus was in the US, but not in prison, he wouldn't know what to do. He'd be scared sick that he would find Brynn and Jacob. He took in the trio of concerned expressions on his teammates' faces, as one by one, they received the same call to report for their mission.

He had wanted to push back, tell the commander he couldn't leave the United States, but if they placed someone new in their unit and shit went sideways, he'd never forgive himself. After all of these years, Scooter's sacrifice was still an empty hole in his gut. He couldn't go through that kind of loss again. Still, the pizza he'd just eaten sat heavy in his churning stomach at the thought of leaving Brynn alone.

He breathed in through his nose, held it, then exhaled. The move to the new house would have to wait. Brynn and Jacob would be safe in the apartment. He would email the Realtor to complete the sale, so when they returned from their mission, they could start packing and move right in. He felt a small squeeze right above his knee. Brynn was gazing up at him, her eyes soft with understanding. She was brave. Reliable. There was no way she would take any kind of chances with Jacob in her care.

Branch cleared his throat. "Sucks, man. Couldn't be worse timing for you. Anything we can help square away, Ransom?"

He shook his head. "Appreciate it." He'd text some of the Teams that would be staying on base. Ask them to drive by occasionally to check on Brynn and Jacob. Maybe he was being paranoid, but he'd been given such a gift by having them enter his life. If they were taken from him, he wouldn't survive it.

Silver shifted, taking his elbow off of the beanbag chair as he sat up. He locked eyes with Neo, and dipped his chin in understanding. "Our intel suggests this mission should be cut and dried. I'm guessing two weeks at most." His gaze drifted to Brynn. "If there is anything you or Jacob need, don't hesitate to call the commander. You'll leave the number, yeah?"

He loved his team for worrying about them, too. They were Neo's, but if anything happened to him on a mission, he had no doubt that the rest of them would step up and make sure Brynn and Jacob were well cared for. "Yeah." He took Brynn's hand, lacing his fingers with hers. "And some of the guys on base. If you need anything or something is bothering you, call one of the numbers I program into your phone."

"Jacob, you're the man of the house while we're gone." Joker ruffled his brother's hair. They had become close in the past week. "That pretty much means listening to whatever Brynn says."

Jacob released a long exasperated sigh, but the pinched expression on his face told him the news was weighing on him. He'd have a heart-to-heart with him when the guys left.

"Guess we should clear out." Branch stood from the recliner. "I want to get a few hours of sleep in before we leave."

The others grunted in agreement and they all rose to their feet.

Silver walked over to where Brynn was now standing in the threshold of the living room. "If you need anything at all, sweet girl, call the commander." Silver pulled Brynn into a bone-crushing hug and made his way to the front door.

Branch followed his lead, hugging her. "It's good to have you and Jacob here. Be safe."

Joker lagged behind, his eyes trained on Brynn. "Can I have a word?" Joker looked over his shoulder, seeking Neo's approval, but she spoke first.

"Of course. Let's talk in the kitchen," she said. He would've told Joker hell no. Whatever he had to say to Brynn could be said in front of him—more because he was aware of Joker's suspicion of women. Brynn must've sensed his hesitation, because she shook her head at him before leading him into the kitchen. The dog looked at him, then toward the kitchen.

"Go ahead and eavesdrop." He scratched Oscar behind the ear, and the dog trotted of behind them.

All he knew was it would be a stupid idea to upset Brynn before a mission, because it would weigh on all of them. She could get angry and leave. He pressed his teeth together, but his jaw relaxed when he heard the words: "I need to apologize." That was a big admission of guilt for Joker. Maybe Brynn and Jacob were helping to heal more than just him.

"Come on, kiddo." He bent and lifted Jacob in his arms. "I'll help you get ready for bed."

CHAPTER EIGHTEEN

BRYNN LEANED AGAINST the kitchen island, the stone counter pressed against her back. Joker stood before her, looking like he'd rather be anywhere else. He rubbed the back of his neck, pieces of his sandy hair falling over his brows. Oscar's nails clicked against the tile as he entered the room and sat at her feet.

"Listen, Brynn." He jammed his hands into his pockets. "I wasn't fair to you that first day at the airport. I was rude. A total prick. I thought you were out to get Neo's money. When he lived back in Boston, women used to come onto him just because of his last name. Everyone knew the Godfreys were loaded. He never had a serious relationship, but women looked at him for one thing: his bank account. When he joined up and moved to Virginia he gained a little bit of anonymity.

"I couldn't care less about Neo's financial situation." She crossed her arms over her chest, and Oscar whined, sensing the growing tension. "That's not true." A sigh escaped her lips. She didn't want to talk about Neo while he was in the other room, but Joker was on edge, and she sensed he needed to get whatever he was going to say off of his chest. "I do care. I care that he has enough to provide for Jacob. If for some reason I wasn't here—"

"Don't say things like that. That man in there"—he pointed toward the living room—"is a damn good one. I've never seen him wrapped up in a woman. Never. But even if you're not right next to him, his eyes are on you. He's got this look..." Joker stopped and cleared his throat. "If you left, he'd be destroyed. Is that what you're planning?" His eyes narrowed.

She pulled back her shoulders. "I have no clue what the future holds, but I'd never intentionally hurt Neo or Jacob."

"Shit. Sorry. Jumping down your throat isn't the best way to apologize."

For the first time, she noticed that Joker looked lost. Perhaps he'd always appeared that way or maybe he was letting her see a side of him he'd concealed before. "I thought the worst." He looked down at his feet and then back up at Brynn. "I don't have a great history with the women in my life. My grandmother always said my mom could've done better than our father. Asked how we could blame her for leaving when we were brats and my father refused to give up the army or his Alaskan homestead. Mom cleared out Dad's bank account when he was on active duty and left us in remote Alaska alone. She said the military lifestyle wasn't what she signed up for, even though she knew full well that our father was a soldier before marrying him. Met a guy—some wealth manager, not even a fraction of the man our father was, but who could give her the lifestyle she wanted. Haven't seen her since the day she drove off on Dad's snowmobile."

"Joker." She dropped her arms to her sides. "You didn't have to tell me that, but I'm sorry. I know how it feels to be rejected by a parent. Both actually."

"After I read the police reports, I was so sure you were playing Neo. Now, just a week later, I feel physically ill for thinking that. Fuck. I'm sorry. Sorry for what that bastard did to you—I don't know the whole story but I know enough. I'm also sorry I sifted through your personal life." His expression was frigid, but it warmed her that he'd get defensive on her behalf.

"Neo didn't tell you?" Oscar pressed against her calves.

"Only that your brother was a monster, and he wanted to keep a close eye on his whereabouts. Said it was your story to tell."

"He abused me as a child. My parents didn't listen, or didn't care when I confided in them. My grandmother got me out." A surprised squeak escaped her lips when Joker pulled her into a hug.

"Fuck. I'm so sorry." He took a step back.

"While I appreciate your apology, I know our situation wasn't exactly planned for. That you might have questions about who I am. You should know that I came to stay with Jacob. I couldn't imagine not having him in my life."

"And what about Ransom?"

Her cheeks tingled as warmth rushed to her face. "Things have gotten complicated."

Neo might not want her discussing their relationship, but he sure wasn't hiding his feelings. He'd wrapped his arm around her in front of his teammates, held her hand, and kissed her hair. With each claiming action, her joy built and grew until its soft glow poured through her.

"I see how you are around Jacob and Ransom. Makes me

remember that people aren't all bad. I have a sister, Addy, she is a super geek. Sweet as all get-out. She's nothing like my mother and neither are you. I'm happy as hell my brother has found himself a good woman. I don't think anyone of us could deny that you and Jacob haven't added some much-needed excitement to our lives." He stepped forward, pulled his hands out of his pockets, and gave her another hug.

"I think you all have more than enough excitement in your lives." Despite the restlessness that had invaded her since Neo and his team were notified, she fought to project confidence, even to Joker.

"Stay safe." How could Joker tell her to stay safe when he was about to enter a hostile environment? "We'll see you in a few weeks."

"Take care of him." She hadn't meant for those words to tumble from her lips, but they had all the same.

"Don't worry, Neo can take care of himself. We all can, but we always have each other's backs. We have yours, too, you know." Joker walked past her and out the door.

She stood there for a moment longer, smoothing Oscar's soft fur, mulling over what Joker had said. Her mouth was bone-dry, and she had been fighting to keep her breathing steady since the call they'd received. Neo didn't need to be worrying about her when his sole focus should be on the upcoming mission and coming home safe. After a few minutes of standing in the kitchen lost in her own thoughts, she went to find Neo and Jacob in the living room. With soft steps, she glided over the wood floors of the apartment and looked in. Neither of them were there, so she went to the room they usually slept in. Jacob was in bed, tucked under the sheets, and Neo was sitting at his side. "When we get called out on a mission, it means we're trying to stop someone who is trying to hurt someone else. Sometimes we're gone for a few weeks or even a month or more. Your uncle Branch seems to think this will be a quick mission, and it might be, but I don't want you to worry. I want you to enjoy school and take care of Brynn. She's special to both of us."

Brynn backed out of the room, eyes burning with tears. She wanted them to have this time to talk, and she needed a shower.

She headed down the hall and into Neo's bedroom. Inside the en suite, she turned on the tap, and water pummeled against tile. Hot water pounded against her as she lathered creamy lavender-scented soap over her skin. Her breasts were sensitive from Neo's attention. He'd tortured her nipples into tight buds, and she hadn't thought anything could feel better. She'd been wrong. Liquid heat gathered in her lower belly. She wanted him, but it would have to wait. There was no way she would distract him from getting the sleep he needed before his mission. She washed her hair, turned off the water, and stepped out of the shower. Her feet sank into the fuzzy mat below her, and she quickly rubbed one of the thick towels over her skin and hair. After knotting the towel against her chest, she turned the doorknob. Steam plumed out of the bathroom on her heels, and she slammed right into a hard, male chest. Instead of taking a step back, she curled her fingers into his shirt. "Sorry," she murmured even though she was not in the least bit sorry for anything that led to him being pressed against her.

"I didn't mean to invade your privacy. Just wanted to check on you. Was everything okay with Joker?"

"Yes. He said he was sorry for being wary of me. I'm glad you have good friends. Is Jacob asleep?"

"Yup. Gave him his meds just like you showed me. The paper on the fridge really helps, too."

"Neo?"

"Yeah, sweetheart?"

"Could you, ah…sleep in here tonight?"

He lowered his head and rested his forehead against hers. "Of course. I don't want you to feel any pressure to do more than sleep, though."

"Is that what you want to do? Sleep?"

"Brynn." The way he ground out her name sent a shiver of pleasure sliding over her skin. "I don't want to rush you. There's time."

She stepped closer until she was up against him, and exactly what he wanted was apparent against the material of her towel.

"It's important that you sleep, but it is a bit earlier than I thought it was. I want you, Neo."

CHAPTER NINETEEN

B RYNN HADN'T EVEN finished saying his name and he was swinging her up into his arms. He crossed the room and deposited her on the bed, climbing up beside her. He lay next to her, running his fingers through her damp hair. The towel had slipped off, and he let out a growl of appreciation at the swell of her coral-tipped breasts, her soft waist, and the flare of her hips. "Once again, I'm the only one here without clothes." Amusement danced in her eyes. Ones that were beyond blue, bordering violet.

He chuckled at her pout. Loved that she teased him. No one had ever teased him before. "Nothing wrong with that." He nipped her earlobe, getting caught up in her playful side.

"There's something very wrong with that." She smiled against his lips, then went up on her knees and tugged his shirt up. He arched his hips and yanked off his jeans, tossing them to the side.

"Better?" He followed her gaze of appreciation as it drifted down his body.

"Mm-hmm."

He kissed her once, then twice. "So fucking sweet." He murmured the words, and when she drew in a quick breath, he licked her bottom lip. She opened immediately, taking everything he offered and giving him back so much more.

Her hands roamed his chest and stomach, making him dizzy like a high-altitude climb. Her fingers wrapped around his length, and he hissed out a breath. Between tasting her essence earlier and having her smooth curves up against his body, he was on edge. "If you keep that up, I'm never going to end up inside you." She shivered against his palms.

"Come here. So damn beautiful. Every inch of you." He sat up with his back against the headboard, lifted her onto his lap, and helped her wrap her legs around his waist. They dove back into the kiss. Her breasts were pressed against his chest, and he could feel the pound of her heart matching his own. She was tipping her hips, desperately seeking out more friction. Her hands were roaming his back, tugging him closer. Everything about having Brynn in his lap was pure heaven, and he hadn't even entered her. When he rolled the peaks of her breasts between his thumb and forefinger, she gasped. He continued on, massaging, licking, touching anywhere he could reach while still keeping her centered on his lap. There was something incredibly intimate about being eye to eye, chest to chest with Brynn. Nothing had ever moved him so profoundly, reached deep inside him and made a fundamental shift in his heart like her.

"Neo." Her tongue swiped against the pulse point in his neck, making him tremble. "Please. I'm ready." Her breath warmed the spot where she'd just licked. He steadied her with one arm and reached for the nightstand drawer with his other. His fingers closed around a foil wrapper. He tore the package with his teeth and ran the condom down his length. Brynn's eyes were fixated on him, her breath quickening.

"Any point you need me to stop, or I'm being too rough,

you tell me."

She nodded, pupils wide and dark.

"Promise."

"Yes." Her voice was breathless as he notched his cock at her center. He pushed in slowly, inch by inch, giving her time to adjust or tell him if she was uncomfortable. Her core gripped him, and she rocked her hips, taking him deep into her wet heat. Fucking bliss. He'd never get enough. He put his hand between them, stroking her arousal. She was starting to tremble beneath his touch, her breath coming in choppy pants. She tightened around him, shaking, his name a breathless whisper breaking from her throat. Her heat pulsed around him, and all he could do was grip her hips as his own orgasm tore through him. She leaned her cheek against his collarbone. Though they were still connected he made no attempt to move. He ran his fingertips up and down her back, and her arms were tangled around his neck. Her skin glowed with a light sheen of sweat, her cheeks flushed with color. *I love you* was on the tip of his tongue. He was desperate to tell her, to beg her to never leave, but he held himself back. When they returned from this mission, he'd tell her how he felt. He didn't want her to think the words were a meaningless result of their lovemaking.

"You fit so perfect against me." He kissed the top of her head, wrapping her cooling body in his embrace. "Didn't hurt you, did I?"

"I'll still be feeling you tomorrow, but not because you hurt me." She tilted her chin up at him. Those pretty lips were curved into a smile. He lowered his head and met her lips, pouring every word he couldn't say into the kiss.

"Going to miss you a hell of a lot," he said when they broke apart.

"Then you'll have to do your best to get back fast." Her words might've been teasing, but her eyes told him everything he needed to know. She glanced away and blinked, clearing the emotion from her eyes. He loved that she was trying so hard to be tough for him. She was tough. He couldn't forget that. It wasn't lost on him that she'd shoulder the weight of being a military spouse with grace. The other day when he went to base to work out with his team, he'd added her as the benefactor to his will. If he died, everything he had would be hers. There wasn't a shred of doubt in his soul that she wouldn't use it to care for Jacob.

Goose bumps were running down her arms. She was getting cold, and he was being greedy holding her for so long. He lifted her off of him and laid her down on the bed. "I'm going to take care of the condom." He drew the comforter up over her soft skin, kissed her cheek, and walked to the bathroom. When he returned, he slipped under the covers beside her. She rolled into his arms and he held her close. Her breath hit his chest in warm puffs, and occasionally she'd press her lips to his skin.

He'd never met another human with a heart as pure as Brynn's. He wanted to hand her the world. To sit together on the back deck of their new home and talk about their days, to laugh with her, watch as she pushed Jacob on the swing, see how her belly rounded with his child. Jacob would be an amazing uncle and Brynn a loving mother.

"Do you want kids?" He hadn't meant to ask, but the picture in his mind of her carrying their baby wouldn't go away. Her back straightened beneath his fingers and she locked eyes with him.

"Yes." She tugged at her bottom lip before asking, "You?"

"Yeah, sweetheart. I do now. Never thought I would. Always seemed like too much risk—maybe I'd end up with a woman like my mother, or maybe I'd be too selfish to give a child the attention they deserved. With you, everything is different. I look in the mirror and see myself becoming the man I want to be. You and Jacob have thawed something, healed something inside me that was still raw."

"Jacob would be an amazing uncle."

"No doubt in my mind. The kid would be busting a gut as we navigated dirty diapers and waking up at all hours of the night."

"I always thought I'd only want one. That if there were more than that, one could turn on the other. I don't feel that way anymore. If they had an ounce of their father's honor, his kindness, they'd never lift a hand to their sibling."

"Nothing that came from you could ever be cruel, Brynn. All you hold inside you is beauty and warmth. You're a nurturer. Even though you're worried about me leaving, you've kept your chin up and reassured me that you're fine. And I know you will be because beneath all that empathy and kindness is strength. I couldn't say steel, because nothing about you is hard. More like the sea. Strong. Enduring. You've been dealt some rough hands, but you always rush back to the shore. You keep going long after others would've quit."

"I think you've built me up in your mind as something

I'm not. I don't want you to wake up one day and realize you've put me on a pedestal that I don't deserve."

"I know exactly who you are, Brynn. I see you. You're not some trophy I want to display. You're real. Someone I can stand beside and know without a doubt that you wouldn't betray me. My equal. A partner I can share everything with. That's how I see you."

Something wet slid down his chest. A tear. He lifted her chin and kissed away the salty trail it had left behind. "I know you'd believe me. If I came to you with a burden, you'd share the weight with me. You'd help fix the problem. Never would you ignore someone hurt or in need. You have no idea how much that means to me."

"Brynn, if I had been in your life when we were kids, if you told me Fergus was hurting you, there would've been nowhere on earth he could hide."

"I know. My whole life I unsuccessfully searched for a place I'd feel safe." Her voice was muffled with exhaustion. "Except I didn't know I wouldn't find it in a place. I found it in you."

Emotion jammed into his throat. "Sleep, sweetheart," he choked out. He didn't deserve her, but he was going to do everything he could to keep her. She was his and he'd shamelessly protect her with everything in his power.

CHAPTER TWENTY

BRYNN HADN'T BEEN prepared for the onslaught of feelings she'd have the day that Neo left. When the door had closed behind him, the soft click of the lock might as well have been a deafening slam. She'd had to sit on the floor for a moment and breathe. For as long as he was away, she would go through the motions. Do what needed to be done. Knowing he was overseas, putting himself in insurmountable danger quaked the ground beneath her. Heavy regret made it impossible to fill her lungs completely, and her belly was a tangle of knots. Why hadn't she told Neo how she felt when he was holding her? When they'd been talking about the future and children?

Her whole life she'd been trying to harden herself against forming relationships, never wanting to be at the will or whim of another. With Neo, though, she laid herself bare, emotionally and physically. He'd put her desires and needs first from the start, and had earned her trust with his actions. Being vulnerable with him was easy. Anything she exposed to him he'd fold into a blanket of protection and keep safe. There was no doubt that the emotion she was feeling was love. The foreign feeling welled up and burned hot and bright inside her. Being without Neo would be hard, but that burn would carry her through.

"All right, Jacob." She checked his backpack one last time. "I think that's everything. I've labeled all your things for your teacher and let him know if there are any questions to call me." She swung the backpack onto her shoulders and straightened Jacob's collared shirt. Since Neo had left, Jacob was more withdrawn.

"I miss him, too." She leaned down and kissed Jacob's forehead. "He wanted to drive you on the first day of school." Brynn crouched down at his side. "Wanted to spend more time with you before he got called on a mission. He will be back, though, Jacob, and when he is, we'll move into the new house. Your brother and probably the entire team will escort you to school. I'm sure Collin is going to be excited to see you today. Maybe Mr. Bloom could connect us with his parents, and we could invite them all over for pizza and a game some night." Jacob turned his head and cast her a small smile. "Okay, then. It's a date." She stood up and rounded the wheelchair, pushing Jacob into the hallway. She closed the door behind her and locked the dead bolt.

"I'm going to stop at the grocery store after I bring you to school. How does macaroni and cheese sound tonight? I don't know about you, but I could use some comfort food." Jacob turned his head to the left, but not with the usual gusto reserved for her homemade mac and cheese or lasagna. "I know this is really hard, but we'll make it through. We always do, and your brother would never abandon us. He's working hard to get home to us as we speak." She pressed the elevator button, and they descended to the first floor. The automatic door opened to a wide, cloudless sky. A sea-scented breeze fluttered through the air as they walked to the

SUV.

Footsteps sounded behind her and she jerked around. The man had appeared out of nowhere, but he had a set of keys in his hand. Another resident at the apartment complex, and she'd nearly jumped out of her skin. She'd been on edge since she discovered Fergus was in the country, and even though she hated to feel like a damsel in distress, without Neo here, a new layer of fear had developed. Proving to herself that she could be brave, she smiled at the stranger.

"Nice morning, huh?" She gripped the handles of Jacob's wheelchair. Maybe she should've just stayed quiet.

Then the man smiled. He looked friendly enough, but even his grin didn't put her at ease. "I was just thinking the same thing. I've seen you coming and going. You live on the floor above me. Haven't seen your husband in a couple days, though. Everything okay?"

She didn't bother to correct him, more than ready to get to the car. "He's around, just busy with work." She wasn't sure what prompted her to lie, but it probably wasn't a good idea to let a stranger know that she and Jacob were alone, no matter how normal he seemed.

"Yeah, I know the feeling. Anyway I am in unit 310 if you need anything. Have a nice morning." The man walked past them and stopped at a sporty BMW.

"Thank you," she said and quickly hit the key fob to open the doors. She lowered the ramp, and after securing Jacob's wheelchair, they made the short drive to the school. It wasn't until she dropped Jacob off and was nearly to the grocery store when a thought hit her. She stiffened, gripped the steering wheel as ice formed in her stomach. Her heart rate picked up as she thought back to what Neo had told her about the apartment complex when she and Jacob moved in.

There were only six units on each floor. The stranger had told her he lived in 310, hadn't he? The fine hairs on the back of her neck stood up, and she looked in her rearview mirror. There were several cars behind her and some in the right lane. She hadn't been paying attention earlier to see if one had been following her because except for the uneasy feeling, she really had nothing to worry about. She was being crazy. Fergus was in prison. She couldn't seem to shake the dread prickling down her back, so she switched into the left lane, paying careful attention to the cars in her mirror.

A beat-up sedan two cars behind her moved as well. Her heart started to hammer. The man she'd spoken to this morning was getting into a BMW. Had he, though? She'd been occupied by Jacob, but she couldn't recall noticing any cars drive past them. She glanced at her cell phone. She'd find a safe spot and call Neo's commander. The sedan moved into the left lane to pass the car behind her. Now he was closer. If he was following her, he wasn't making any effort to hide it. The man behind the wheel was bald and older, like the man in the parking lot. Why hadn't she paid better attention to his appearance? Why had she engaged with him at all?

She shifted back into the left lane. The sedan did the same. There was a tingling in her hands and feet. Something was not right. What would Neo want her to do? Who was this man and what did he want from her? Or perhaps she was losing the battle with some kind of undiagnosed mood disorder. There was no reason someone would want to hurt her, save for Fergus. She fought to expand her shallow breaths, but her lungs burned in protest. Her knuckles were white against the steering wheel. She needed to calm her heart, or she was going to pass out. Get off the road. Find a police station or hospital. She could run inside and call for help.

Without bothering to flick on her directional, she shifted hard, crossing the lanes and narrowly missing the exit. With trembling hands, she touched the voice-activated search on her GPS. Thank goodness. There was a police station only a mile away. The sedan had taken the same exit. The man waved at her and pointed to the side of the road. Were her tail lights out? Was he just a good Samaritan? Maybe he was trying to tell her something was wrong with the van. Thoughts flew through her head like rapid fire as hysteria clawed up her throat, choking her. She glanced at the map on the GPS. Almost there. The man kept gesturing to her, but she didn't intend to stop.

Neo had programmed several phone numbers into her cell. She fumbled with the search feature. With the way her hands were shaking, there was no way she could scroll down to the numbers. Her heartbeat had taken on a strange rhythm, as though the organ was beating outside of her chest. The hood of the sedan was mere inches from her bumper, but the police station was just up ahead. Following the GPS instructions, she took a left and realized instantly that she'd made a terrible mistake. The road before her was a desolate side street, lined with thick trees. It might lead to the police station, but the person behind her had a lot of opportunity if he wanted to hurt her. She couldn't get enough oxygen into her lungs as the car sped up on her tail. Using the voice search, she called up the commander's phone number. She squeezed the wheel as it rang once, then twice. The call went to voice mail. "This is Brynn-n..." she stammered. "I work for Neo Godfrey—R-Ransom. I think I'm being—" She didn't get another word out before the sedan careened into the SUV.

"Everything's going be okay. Everything's going be okay." She did her best to grip the wheel and stay on the road. The vehicle she was driving was much bigger than a sedan. Did he really think he could run her off the road? He must've come to the same conclusion, because suddenly there was something flashing in his hand. Something sounded behind her—like balloons popping. Glass shattered and adrenaline drenched her system. Thank God she'd dropped Jacob off at school. He'd be taken care of until Neo returned from his mission.

There was another pop and the car tipped to the right. The air pressure gauge lit up on the display screen. She pressed on the gas, desperate to get out of the situation, but the car spun and hit a tree. Something exploded by her head, and shattered shards of glass rained down on her. Warmth trickled over her face.

"I'm going to die," she whispered.

She hadn't even told Neo that she loved him. Would he ever find her body or would he think she'd abandoned him like everyone else had? The car creaked or maybe it was the tree she'd crashed into. There was a deafening crack, and whatever was holding the SUV in place broke free. The vehicle began to roll down the embankment. A scream was caught in her throat. Her body tossed and jolted with the car. Something smashed into her head and there was pressure in her hip, but she couldn't feel any pain. Finally, something stopped the car's forward motion, leaving her hanging upside down.

The scent of gasoline hit the air and smoke billowed from the front of the car. Tiny flames erupted and danced along the hood. She needed to get out. The glint of steel drew her gaze. Scooter's dog tags dangled against the shattered mirror. She reached up, her fingers closing over metal. A rush of hope and determination slid through her. With the tags in one hand, she clicked frantically at the seat belt release with the other, and finally it unlatched. She dropped onto her neck, folding at an awkward angle. The steel frame was crushed on the driver's side, making the window inaccessible.

She dragged herself across the roof to the passenger-side window. The edge was lined with jagged glass, but she didn't have a choice. She pulled herself through the tiny opening. Her legs didn't seem to be working, so she used her elbows to wiggle away from the vehicle, only she was still on a slope. Her body started to slide downward, driven by gravity. She dug her fingers into the ground, but the incline was too steep.

Her nails ripped off as she desperately clawed against the side of the hill. Blood coated her hands, and she continued to tumble out of control. She wished she'd been stronger, smart enough to save herself. Finally, she slammed into a rock and heard a loud crack. She worried she'd broken several bones, but before she could gather her wits, an earth-shaking roar rocked her. Heat blasted against her face and flames shot over her. If she hadn't moved through the car window, she would've been blown to pieces. Her ears rang and her vision wavered. Dark closed in and she was falling again.

CHAPTER TWENTY-ONE

NEO LEANED BACK in the hard metal seat of the helicopter. The headset over his ears crackled as the pilot announced their descent. Branch had been right. The mission had been cut and dried, in and out. They gone in and eliminated the root of the terrorist organization, then made it to their rallying point without any interference. Even the dip and sway of the aircraft and the weightless feeling in his gut as the chopper dropped didn't bother him. He was missing Brynn and Jacob. Couldn't wait to burst through the front door and wrap them in a hug. The scent of fuel, sweat, and antiseptic filled the aircraft. They had cleaned up some grazes and surface injuries with the wipes they carried. The team would have to report to the commander on base and debrief. He was itching to undo the heavy straps around his shoulders, anchoring him to the seat.

"Shit, Ransom. You got ants in your pants or something?" Silver said into the headset. He elbowed the older man beside him.

"You would, too, if you had someone waiting for you at home, old man," Joker piped up. Branch had his head tipped back, eyes closed, and although they couldn't hear him with the headphones on, he was sure his teammate was sawing wood. Branch was constantly voted worst snorer among the team.

The blades sliced through the air with a noisy whine as the chopper landed inside the chain-link perimeter of the base. Once the skids bumped against the ground, he discarded the headset and tore off his seat belt. Being confined to the enclosed space had never been his favorite thing, and now the anticipation of seeing his family overrode everything else. His family. Something he never imagined in a million years he'd have, let alone cherish. The word used to conjure nothing inside him. It was a blank, empty word. One of numbness and envy. Now, the word evoked images of Brynn and Jacob. A place of support and connection. A life outside the Teams. Wind whipped through the door as they jumped out onto the tarmac and snuck inside his sweat-dampened shirt. His boots slapped against the wet pavement as he and his team headed to debrief. Rain lashed around them, and he pulled his cap down lower over his forehead.

Despite the dark, the floodlights surrounding the main building broke through the shadows, highlighting his commander's form. Anxiety tightened his chest as the man began to jog toward them. A prickle of unease swept over his scalp, and he started to run, feet pounding against the solid ground. The wind and rain that had made him cold upon landing evaporated and suddenly he was a roaring furnace. Something was wrong. He could feel it in his bones.

"Ransom," the commander barked. "Conference room." The man didn't wait for confirmation, but hurried out of the rain. He cast a glance over his shoulder. His team was right at his back, just where they always were, and he was grateful.

The commander held open the door of the concrete

building and walked briskly down the hall. The man's shoulders were tight, his neck corded, setting off warning bells in Neo's head. Lt. Commander Richardson plowed through the door of the conference room, and the team filtered in around him.

Beneath the florescent lights, the commander's lips were set in a tight line. "I received a voice mail this morning." The entire team was around them, but the commander addressed him directly. His pulse began to quicken. "I was in a meeting with the governor, and I missed the call. You need to hear it. Brace, Ransom." The commander put his phone in the middle of the conference table and turned it on speaker. His team was silent, all eyes trained on the phone. He gripped the chair in front of him, fingers digging into the upholstery.

"This is Brynn." Her breathless voice laced with terror nearly brought him to his knees. "I work for Neo Godfrey—R-Ransom. I think I'm being—"

Her voice was cut off by a loud crash, but the call was still being recorded. Metal scraping against metal flooded the line. Tires screeching on pavement. Brynn's labored breaths spiked sickening fear into his gut. She was whispering, "Everything's gonna be okay. Everything's gonna be okay." He bowed his head, unable to breathe. Then came the gunshots. Glass shattering. A terrified scream. There was a crack that made the whole boardroom seem to shake, followed by another harrowing whisper. "I'm going to die." *No. Don't, sweetheart. Christ, don't.* He hated the conviction and resignation in her voice. There was a series of thuds, as though the car was tumbling over a cliff. The sound of flesh pounding into something solid had bile flooding his throat.

Then silence. The car must've stop moving. *Please, Brynn. Please.* Each sound he'd listened to was acid eating away at his insides, but he'd shoulder it if he could hear some sign of life. Her breath, her voice. *Goddamn it.* Time had no relevance—it could've been minutes or seconds. He was clutched in fear, and then he heard some wrestling, the click of a seat belt. A thud and then breathing. Thank fuck there was more breathing. Glass being crushed, the crunch of leaves. The sound faded and a whoosh filled the line. Then there was silence. Neo barely made it to the trash can. Vomit burned up his throat and filled his mouth.

His team was standing around the table in stunned silence.

"Fuck!" he cried, and the scream echoed around the room. Seemed to shake the foundation of the building. Or maybe it was him shaking.

His insides were quivering. "What the hell was that?" He spun around to the commander. "Please tell me you found her." He raked his hands over his scalp. "Was Jacob with her? Where the hell is she now? Fuck, I never should've left."

Silver was pacing across the room. He barely registered the heavy hand on his shoulder.

"The crash happened this morning," the commander said as Silver gripped him more tightly. "I've had law enforcement keep me up to date. So far, the timeline is she dropped Jacob off at school and was driving on a low-traffic road. Tire tracks show two cars. One was the aggressor. Shell casings were found all over the scene. The audio makes it sound like Brynn might've escaped before the explosion, but we haven't been able to find any trace of her. I'm sorry."

"She's alive. I know it," he bit out. How dare the commander suggest otherwise. He balled his hands into tight fists.

"Ransom." The commander's tone was laced with sympathy and understanding. "Kills me to say it, but if she got out of that car alive, she would've had to travel a hell of a long way out of the range of the explosion. They heard the blast from the police station up the street. Emergency response was there within minutes. No one saw anyone meeting Brynn's description. By the time they got control over the blaze, it was pouring. Search and Rescue combed the area, but nothing was found."

His chest was heaving. The room blurred and tilted.

Silver pounded a hand on his back. "Breathe. You're no help to Brynn if you pass out."

He blew out a series of quick breaths, trying to leash his emotions. "Where is my brother now?" He could barely whisper the words.

"He's here. In my office. The school nurse sent home his medications, and one of the medics on base has already given him his evening doses. I tried to talk to him, but he hasn't made any indication that he's listening. Hasn't made a sound, but there's tears on his cheeks every time I go in."

"Of course he hasn't." Joker was eating up the floor in quick, purposeful strides. "He's probably scared out of his mind. Sitting alone in your fucking office."

Joker swung open the conference room door, then turned to him. "I'll go check on Jacob. Focus on finding Brynn."

"Respect, sir, but if anyone could survive a catastrophic

accident, it would be this woman. Been through hell. Tough as a SEAL." Branch wore the hardened expression he reserved for battle. It was odd to see it on his face stateside. He was the most affable of the bunch.

"We're gonna find her, Ransom." Silver's large hand came to rest on the back of his neck. "There's no other option."

The commander gave a curt nod. "Does Brynn have any enemies? Crossed my mind that if someone ran her off the road, maybe they snatched her when she climbed out of the vehicle."

Neo swore as a thousand horrific scenarios bombarded him. "Is someone looking into the traffic cameras?"

"Yes, the nerds in tech are on it." The commander pulled out a chair and sat at the conference table. "If there was a police station at the end of the road, she might've been trying to get help. She knew someone was following her."

Neo's blood ran cold. "Her brother is at Walpole in Massachusetts."

The commander pushed up his sleeves, jaw set. "Got a contact up there in corrections that owes me a marker. Let's reach out, see what I can dig up."

"Thank you, sir." He paced the end of the room, even when Branch and Silver sat at the conference table. He couldn't sit, not when it felt as though worms were crawling and twisting under his skin.

The commander put his phone on speaker, leaned back in his chair, and steepled his hands. The other line rang once then twice. A gruff voice filled the conference room. "Chief Howard. It's the middle of the night. Better be important."

"Lt. Commander Richardson. We need information on Fergus Yarrow, an inmate in your facility. We need it now," he said, voice steady but rigid.

"That sick bastard?" The chief's tone was now alert. "Second time I've heard his name this week. A report came across my desk that he tried to choke one of the therapy dogs from the canine programs."

"We believe he might've played a role in a woman's accident today." He hated not knowing what had happened. Hated that he was still in this room and not out searching for her. "We need answers now."

"I'll radio down and have one of the guards pull him into interrogation. Unfortunately, I can't follow the old methods, but I'll try to breathe some fear into him. We'll search his cell and see if he's contacted anyone recently."

"Call us back when you have some information." The commander hung up. "I just sent you the location of the crash site, Ransom. An officer is monitoring the crime scene. I'll call the station and let them know to expect you at the scene."

"Thank you, sir. I need to tell my brother what's going on." His team stood up, their footfalls behind him as he walked out of the room. He rushed down the hall, rage burning in his chest.

"She's strong. Don't forget that," Silver said from behind him.

"You can only be so strong when you're faced with bullets and a fucking explosion." She couldn't be dead. Not when he'd just found her. He'd rescued thousands of civilians throughout the years, yet he hadn't been able to protect the one who mattered most.

They rounded the corner to the offices and spotted Joker huddled close to Jacob. He couldn't cross the room fast enough and threw his arms around his brother's shoulders. Jacob's cheeks were wet, and his eyes red. He pressed his forehead against Jacob's. Tears burned and clouded his eyes, before he leaned back and swiped them away. "I'm going to find her, Jacob. I will bring her home. Will you be okay with Joker?"

Jacob turned his head. The poor kid was exhausted and terrified but was being brave enough to stay with his teammate.

"Stay strong. We're going to bring her back." The words tasted sour in his mouth, and he wished he hadn't made that promise. What if the worst had happened? How would he explain it to his brother?

Branch seemed to sense what he was thinking, because he came up behind him and clapped his back. "Let's move out."

THE LOCATION OF the crash was about twenty minutes from the base. Brynn might've been driving to the mall or maybe a grocery store, then took an exit when she realized someone was following her. The road was the perfect place for an ambush, lined with trees and a steep embankment on either side. The moment Brynn turned onto the street she would've known she was in trouble. She must've been so scared. He never should've left the States. If he'd listened to his gut and got Jacob and Brynn situated in the new home before going on a mission, they might still be safe. Silver pulled his SUV alongside the blue and white patrol car parked on the side of the road and rolled down the automatic window. From the passenger's seat, he barely noticed the heavy rainfall blowing into the front seat of the vehicle.

"Your commander called ahead. You're clear to search the area," a clean-shaven patrolman yelled over the storm. They'd brought night-vision goggles and military-grade flashlights to search the area. The moment they were parked, he unbuckled his seat belt and slid to the ground. The stream from his flashlight caught the glint of steel. He stepped closer to the embankment and nearly dropped to his knees. There was nothing left of the car except for two stark tangles of metal.

"No one would've survived within twenty feet of a blast like that." He hadn't realized he said the words out loud until Branch growled beside him.

"Get your shit sorted, Ransom. Brynn's out there being tough for you. Show her the same respect."

His teammate was right. He locked down his spiraling emotions and started the desperate search for the woman he loved. She could be gravely injured, and every moment that passed was one that her life could be slipping away. From him and from Jacob.

CHAPTER TWENTY-TWO

BREATHING HURT. HELL, everything hurt. Brynn was lucky to be alive; now she just had to find help. She'd lost feeling in her elbows and belly long ago, but could tell they were bleeding as she dragged herself over the forest floor because dried leaves and twigs stuck to her like magnets. Now that it was raining, all of her was soaked anyway. She cataloged her injuries as she crawled. At least one of her legs was broken. The return of feeling to lower extremities was bittersweet. She was shaking with pain but, at least for now, she still had sensation in her legs. She just couldn't put weight on the left without a gut-wrenching slide of bone-on-bone pain in her femur. After the explosion, she must've lost consciousness. The blast had knocked her off the rock she'd fallen on, tossing her to the bottom of the embankment.

When she came to, it was dark, windy, and drizzling. The only light was the SUV at the top of the cliff. She had made it far enough away from the scene of the crash that the flames had disappeared, as had the rock-laden ridge. A shiver racked her body. She had no idea how long she'd been out here, but fear drove her forward. What if the man who'd run her off the road came back to finish the job? Or worse, went after Jacob? She had to get herself medical attention and warn someone to protect Jacob. Thank God he'd been at school before the crash. Even thinking of him inside the car with her made her dizzy.

She'd thought she was going to die in the crash, but she'd survived not only the accident but also a fifty-foot roll. There was no way she was going to give up. She fingered the dog tags that were still tangled around her fingers. It was a miracle she hadn't let go of them during the fall. As she squeezed the metal, Neo's words replayed in her head. *No matter what situation I'm in, I will not give up.* She pushed forward. One elbow, then the next. Fire burned in her lungs with every intake of breath. At best it was cracked ribs; at worst it was a punctured lung. Her elbow landed on a rock, and she bit back a scream. Her eyes burned, but she was too dehydrated for tears. *Even if I wished I were dead, I'd fight until my last breath.* One elbow, then the next. She dragged forward another inch. She clutched the dog tags and gritted her teeth. *Because anything else would tarnish Scooter's memory.*

Her eyes widened as the tags caught a stream of light. She glanced to her left. There was a fire up ahead. Had she been crawling in circles? Was it the enflamed SUV? She inched forward, wheezing from the exertion, and heard a laugh. It was a woman's—pretty and bright. She paused to catch her breath, and a guitar chord rang through the forest. An angel's voice poured out through the night. The sound blanketed around Brynn, and she crawled toward the light and sound. Maybe she really was dying. Her vision was starting to blur, throat so dry it was hard to breathe. *No matter what situation I'm in, I will not give up.* She repeated Neo's words over and over again. Until a high-pitched scream broke through the dark.

"Oh my God, oh my God." Twigs cracked as footsteps rustled over the ground. Something smaller ran up beside her and licked her face. Too small to be Oscar. "Holy shit." The person was down on her knees, but even with the glow of the fire, she couldn't focus on the face. "I'm Samantha Campbell. I'm going to help you. Where are you hurt? I'd like to lift you to my tent, but I don't want to hurt you more."

"You're the voice."

"Maybe. I was singing."

"Brynn Yarrow. Not much else you can hurt."

"Okay, then."

Hands braced beneath her arms, and the woman struggled to drag her toward the tent. All she could do was grit her teeth and hang on to Scooter's tags. She was drained of energy, but somehow she knew the woman with the angel's voice wouldn't harm her. Finally, she was being lifted through the opening and slid onto something soft.

"Oh, you poor sweet thing," the woman cooed. "I'm so glad you stumbled on my campsite. I almost packed up early today because of the rain. Do you think you could drink a bit of water? Then I'll call for help." She probably looked like hell, but the woman didn't flinch at her state, or the blood that was guaranteed to be dripping over her belongings. Samantha cupped the back of her head and lifted a bottle to her lips. The water passed her cracked lips and stung her throat. It was hard to swallow. She took another small sip. The liquid went down easier this time.

"Probably best just to have a little at a time. I'm going to call now."

The small animal, some kind of wiry canine, nudged her hand. Her eyelids drooped. So tired. She was safe now. Safe with this woman, Samantha—and Scooter's dog tags.

⭐

BRYNN BLINKED AGAINST a bright light and slowly opened her eyes. She was lying in a hospital bed. The air was a stale combination of latex and bland food. There were floral arrangements lined against the windowsill—a garden of color in the form of roses, daisies, and a few she didn't recognize. A metal IV stand was beside her bed. A bag was hung from the frame filled with clear liquid that attached to a line in her arm. She moved slightly and the IV pinched at her inner elbow. Her muscles were knotted, but something prevented her from shifting in the bed. She looked down. Neo. There was a feeling of weightlessness in her chest. He was home.

"Neo." His name came out as a broken wheeze. His head snapped up and those beautiful bottle-green eyes met hers. They widened and filled, tears spilling freely over his lower lids.

"Brynn. Thank God." He shifted his chair so he was closer to her face. "Christ, you scared the hell out of me. I thought—fuck. I thought you were gone. Thought I'd have to go home and tell Jacob that the woman who's at the center of both of our worlds wouldn't be walking through the front door. Even the dog's been a mess." He smiled through his tears, but made no move to wipe them away.

"Jacob. Where is he? Is he all right?" The machine at her bedside beeped.

"Whoa there. Try to relax, sweetheart. Yeah. He's at the apartment with the team. They stayed over the past two nights to be with him and take care of Oscar."

"Two nights?" She tried to sit up. An involuntary response to the shock.

"Brynn, you were in really bad shape when you got here. Silver, Branch, and I searched the forest for hours. We went miles into the woods, but somehow you had gone even farther. Dragging yourself across rocks and branches. So strong, sweetheart. Thank you for being so goddamn tough. When I think of what could've happened…" Neo glanced away from her, jaw clenched.

"Hey. Everything's okay now," she croaked.

He let out a quiet chuff. "You're the patient, yet you're reassuring me. Here," he said, lifting a white Styrofoam hospital cup. "Have a few sips, and then we can talk when you're ready."

She parted her lips, and Neo slid the straw into her mouth. She took a small sip, then another. Drinking didn't hurt as much is it had in the woman's tent. "I'm ready to talk now. You were with me. You and Scooter. His dog tags grounded me. When I was crawling, I kept hearing your voice. The things you said about fighting no matter what. Those things gave me the strength I needed to push forward."

He bowed his head, and his shoulders shook silently for a few moments. He sat up and scrubbed his hands over his face. "You still had the tags when they found you at that campsite. Holding on so tight to them the paramedics could hardly get them out of your hands."

"What about Samantha?" She couldn't picture the woman's face, but knew without her help, she might be dead.

"Was that the camper's name?" Neo cupped her hand, rubbing circles over her skin.

"Yes. I forgot her last name, but yes." There had been a tent, and an outdoor fire fighting to stay burning amid the rain.

"She insisted on taking the ambulance with you. Guess she had a purse-sized dog but still pushed her way in. They made her sit in the front. The last nurse said she stayed with you until I got here." He lowered his head and kissed her hand.

"I'd love to contact her." The woman's voice had led her to safety. "Thank her, when I get out of here."

"I'd like to thank her, too."

"So," she sighed. "What's the damage?"

He frowned and closed his hand more tightly around hers. "Broken femur, concussion, four cracked ribs, and a punctured lung. You needed stiches along your stomach from when you dragged yourself out the car window. There was glass embedded there, along with debris from the ground. They were able to set your leg and cast it. You've been on some heavy pain meds to curb the discomfort."

"I guess that explains why I was out so long." She was ready to go back to the apartment to see Neo and Oscar. To sleep with Neo's arms around her. "Thank you for searching for me. For being here."

"Thank you for being brave. For escaping that car before it exploded. I couldn't have lived my life if something happened to you. I would've cared for my brother, but something in me would've died with you. You are everything I never knew I needed." He stroked his thumb over her cheekbone, catching a silent tear that slipped from her eye.

"When I figured out I was in trouble, the thing I regretted the most was not telling you how I felt. I held back, because everything is so new, but I know what I'm feeling. I love you, Neo. You're all the things I admire most in a person. Honorable. Fair. Kind. You stick up for those who need help the most. You've seen the worst of the worst, and yet you have so much love inside you. Love you give so freely."

Neo's eyes brightened and he stood up, moving to brush his hands over her hair. "I love you, too, Brynn. I almost told you on our last night together, but I didn't want to scare you. You and Jacob are my family. My home. Everything that has ever mattered. We're going to move into the new house, us and that smelly dog of yours. I can't wait to have the privilege of holding you every night. Of waking up early to run with Jacob and coming back to make you your morning coffee. I will always trust you, Brynn. Always believe in you. I will do my best to protect you and make you happy."

"We'll keep each other happy and we'll make our house a home for us, the dog, and those smelly teammates of yours." They both chuckled as she threw his words back at him. "I've grown quite fond of them. You're a charming bunch, all of you."

"They've been worried sick, too. You wouldn't believe how they rallied around me and Jacob. How they insisted to the commander that you were strong and could survive something like that." He placed a kiss where his hand had just been on her forehead.

"Neo, someone intentionally ran me off the road. Shot at me. I think it might have to do with Fergus, but I don't understand how that's possible." New fear expanded in her stomach. How could she forget the danger she was in?

"I know, sweetheart. They'll never hurt you again. In the two days you've been out, the team's been hunting. When we learned what happened, our first thought was Fergus. The commander pulled some strings, and your brother was brought into an interrogation room in the middle of the night. He didn't admit to anything, but the guards searched his room and intercepted a letter to a man named Ronald Glen. Someone fitting his description was reported stealing a car a half a mile from our apartment complex, and guess who was the first person to ID him?"

"Who?" Relief swept through her.

"Jacob. The security cameras at the apartment showed you speaking to a man in the parking lot, but there wasn't a clear picture of his face. With the connection to Fergus and the proximity to the apartment, law enforcement showed Jacob a series of pictures. Mr. Bloom and a child psychologist were present when they asked if he'd seen one of the men in the pictures. Jacob turned his head in response to Glen each time. We got lucky, and Glen got pulled over for speeding near Virginia state lines. The car came up as stolen, so he was arrested. He had a photograph of you in his wallet, and more damning information on his phone. He's going to jail. Glen and Fergus don't exist for you anymore. We're going to make sure neither of them ever see outside the walls of prison."

She gripped his hand. "So it's really over." She sighed. "I can't say I'm surprised Jacob made the ID. He's very observant, always taking in his environment. I'm proud of him."

"Me, too."

"I love you," she said, gazing up in his eyes and warming with the love that reflected back at her.

"I love you, too, Brynn. Always."

EPILOGUE

Jacob's laughter rang out from the swimming pool. Joker was in the water with him, spinning him around and around in a donut-shaped float, and the kid was loving every minute of it. Brynn was sitting with him in a lounge chair at the edge of the water, tucked into the V of his thighs, with her back pressed against his chest. She still had the large cast on her left leg, but that would be removed in a few more weeks. Silver was cooking burgers on the grill, and Branch was tossing a red frisbee to Oscar. Every so often, the dog would drop the toy and rush over to the grill to peek at the burgers, then visit the lounge chair to give Brynn a lick before going back to his game of catch.

"Never imagined I'd have all this. My heart's so full, sometimes the thought of losing it shakes the ground under me." The thought of anything happening to Brynn or Jacob, to his team, was enough to make him wake with the sheets stuck to his sweat-soaked skin. He'd never had so much to lose. It was terrifying and humbling.

"You're not going to lose any of it." Brynn squeezed his knee. "None of us are, because no matter what situation we're in, we'll keep fighting." Scooter's tags were now displayed in a shadow box on their mantel. Above it hung a long oak plank with the words *Always Keep Fighting* scrolled across the distressed wood. Painted along the bottom of the sign was a field of poppies. Her nana and Scooter keeping watch over them. A way to keep their memories close and show them what their sacrifices had built. "Look around us. This is a family worth fighting for."

"I can't wait to watch it grow. I want my teammates to find women who they can't imagine living without. I want them to experience the love we have for themselves. Someday soon, we'll add a few kids to the mix. And they'll raise hell, running around this backyard pushing Uncle Jacob in his chair. They'll all drag muddy footprints inside the house."

Brynn dropped her head back and angled her face up to him. A wry smile played on her lips. "How soon?"

He lowered his head to brush his lips over hers. "I don't see any reason to wait," he said against her soft skin. "Do you?"

"I can't think of a single one." Neo slipped his tongue past her lips, pouring all of his love into the kiss. Tomorrow morning, he and Jacob had a surprise for Brynn. Jacob's teacher had introduced a new device at school. His brother could turn his head to select different words or sentences on a tablet. Brynn hadn't seen him use it yet, but tomorrow, Jacob was going to use the device to let her know that Neo had an important question for her. The ring had been burning a hole in his pocket for the past week. It was time to make this family official.

The End

COMING SOON

JULIAN "JOKER" DESMOND sat in a shadowy corner of the bar and nursed his second beer. He wasn't looking to get laid. Picking up women had long ago lost its appeal. There was a dropping sensation in his gut. A loneliness that had intensified over the years. News of his friend Ransom's engagement seemed to highlight the fact that he was alone. Sure, he was happy for Brynn and Ransom. Thrilled even. He loved the woman like a sister now, and she'd brought Jacob into their lives, which was a blessing in itself. Still, he couldn't help but feel a stab of envy.

He'd never have what they had, because since the day his mother left him and his sister in the rural Alaskan bush, he'd known real, enduring love didn't exist. Not for him. He'd never built his life around someone only to watch them walk away like his mother had. Still, he was worried. An emptiness had settled around him. A numbness that permeated his soul. He took a sip of his now-room-temperature beer and narrowed his eyes at the petite blonde stepping on the small stage at the back of the bar. She sat on a high stool, guitar in her lap, and strummed a few chords, tuning the instrument. The crowd didn't seem to bother her, nor did the suggestive calls from some rowdy locals in the back of the room. The bar manager brought a microphone onto the stage and positioned it on a stand in front of her.

"Happy to introduce Sam Campbell. She'll be taking requests until midnight."

The woman smiled at the room, casting a warm glow in the otherwise dingy setting. Guitar chords filled the room, confident and warm, just like her grin. And then she began to sing. A lump formed in his throat as he lost himself in the music. She poured her heart into every note. She was so beautiful, a little angel perched on a pedestal, singing away the worries of the world. Julian was a stark contrast to the woman in front of him, and still, he found himself grabbing a seat closer to the stage, as many of the bar patrons had done. He dealt death and darkness for America's foes, while the woman crooning before him seemed to breathe new life into every person enraptured by her song. She was light, beauty, and life. He'd never have something so refreshing and pure for himself. He didn't deserve the attention of a woman like her, but that didn't keep him from wanting some of her light, if only for a moment, all to himself.

If you enjoyed *Sworn to Lead*,
you'll love the other books in the...

Sworn Navy SEALs series

Book 1: *Sworn to Lead*

Book 2: *Sworn to Honor*
Coming soon!

Available now at your favorite online retailer!

More books by Charlee James

Northampton Hearts series

Book 1: *Twelve Dates of Christmas*

Book 2: *Fourteen Days of Valentines*

Book 3: *Six Days of Spring*

Home Sweet Christmas

The Cape Cod Shore series

Book 1: *In with the Tide*

Book 2: *Caught in the Current*

Book 3: *Dangerous Water*

Available now at your favorite online retailer!

About the Author

Contemporary Romance Author Charlee James was introduced to a life-long love of reading listening to her parents recite nightly stories to her and her older sister. Inspired by the incredible imaginations of authors like Bill Peet, Charlee could often be found crafting her own tales. As a teenager, she got her hands on a romance novel and was instantly hooked by the genre.

After graduating from Johnson & Wales University, her early career as a wedding planner gave her first-hand experience with couples who had gone the distance for love. Always fascinated by family dynamics, Charlee began writing heartwarming novels with happily-ever-afters.

Charlee is a New England native who lives with her husband, daughter, two rambunctious dogs, a cat, and numerous reptiles. When she's not spending time with her tight-knit family, she enjoys curling up with a book, practicing yoga, and collecting Boston Terrier knick-knacks.

Thank you for reading

Sworn to Lead

If you enjoyed this book, you can find more from all our great authors at TulePublishing.com, or from your favorite online retailer.